"I'm glad I came back, Kirk. I missed your family. And you."

He swallowed. Everything in him wanted to shout from the mountain peaks that he'd never stopped loving her. But his spirit still nudged him to wait.

Callie grinned. "Aren't you going to say anything?"

"I'm glad you're back." The words slipped from his lips without hesitancy. He wanted to say more, but for now that was enough.

She nodded as she unhooked Princess from the tree. "I suppose we should go back and pass around a few hugs to the family. See if anyone needs anything."

He helped her climb into the saddle, then hopped onto Charity. He liked the way she'd said that, as if they were her family, too.

Because they were—or they would be, as soon as she would have him.

JENNIFER JOHNSON

and her unbelievably supportive husband, Albert, are happily married and raising three daughters: Brooke, Hayley and Allie. Besides being a middle-school teacher, Jennifer loves to read, write and chauffeur her girls. She is a member of American Christian Fiction Writers. Blessed beyond measure, Jennifer hopes to always think like a child—bigger than imaginable and with complete faith.

JENNIFER JOHNSON

A Heart Healed

Recycling programs for this product may not exist in your area.

ISBN-13: 978-0-373-48655-7

A HEART HEALED

This edition published by arrangement with Love Inspired Books.

www.LoveInspiredBooks.com

Printed in U.S.A.

The Lord is good, a refuge in times of trouble.
He cares for those who trust in him.
—*Nahum* 1:7

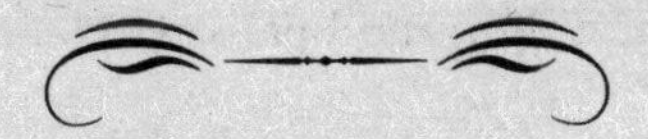

This book is dedicated to Chip MacGregor,
literary agent extraordinaire! Thanks for believing
in my writing, encouraging me toward excellence
and working to get the best contract.
You are a gem, and I praise God for you.

Chapter 1

Kirk Jacobs yanked off his ball cap, wiped the sweat from his forehead and peered down at his sister. "There was only one woman for me. Only one. And she died five years ago."

Pamela placed her hands on her hips. "She did not die, Kirk. She moved away and got married."

After planting the cap back on his head, he lifted both hands. "Married. Died. What's the difference?"

Trying to ignore his sister's glare, Kirk hefted himself onto the tractor seat. Surveying the farm in one quick glance, he sucked in a breath, acknowledging the work he had yet to do. It was more than a man could complete in a day, but Kirk liked it that way. A fellow couldn't think random thoughts when his hands stayed busy. And if his mind did happen to wander to places it ought not to go, he'd hum one of his favorite hymns or try to remember a bit of scripture.

He led a hard life, but a simple one. He shared a good-size house with his twenty-year-old brother, Ben. Until Ben headed off to the university in the fall, anyway. Two years at the community college wasn't enough for his little brother. Ben wanted to go to the University of Tennessee and get his four-year degree in engineering, of all things.

When he moved out, Kirk would be up to his eye-brows in work. In the years since his dad retired, the brothers had carried the heaviest load, caring for the cat-tle and the cornfields. They also tended the strawberry and pumpkin patches as well as the apple and peach or-chard that provided their community with fresh produce in the summer and fall months.

The rest of the family stayed busy, as well. His mom and dad ran the family's bed-and-breakfast, grew a small garden and oversaw the family fun activity cen-ter that ran from May to late October. His sister and her two daughters took care of the gift shop and the small café that served lunch during the activity center's open months.

It was a lot of work, but they had a great family in an ideal situation. The Lord blessed them and showed them how to overcome obstacles. All in all, he couldn't imagine what more a man could want.

"There's a big difference between marriage and death, you big oaf." Pamela swatted at his pant leg. "You gotta quit talking about Callie like that. It creeps me out."

Frustration bubbled up in his gut. "I *don't* talk about her," he snapped. "When someone forces me, I simply acknowledge what she is in my mind. Dead to me."

His retort came out harsher than he intended, and

he knew he should apologize, but Pamela had already crossed her arms in front of her chest and said evenly, "Mom has hired a woman to help out with the fun center and the café. Evidently a young, pretty woman. Said the gal's a lost soul, and Mom wants you—" Pamela reached up and poked his arm "—big brother, to show her around after supper tonight."

Kirk growled. "Why? Does she expect me to fall head over heels for the girl? I'm tired of her matchmaking. If I want a woman, I can find one on my own."

"Now, wait just a minute." She lifted her pointer finger. "First off, Mom never tries to match you with anybody." She lifted her middle finger. "And second, I'm just the messenger. If you don't want to show the girl around, you'll have to take it up with Mom."

"I'll do just that."

Pamela opened her mouth to add something else, but he started the tractor, causing it to roar to life and his sister to take a step back. Just to be sure she knew what an annoyance she was, he shooed her a little farther away then turned the tractor away from her. Her mouth continued to move, no doubt badgering him further, but he ignored her and made his way into the fields.

He assumed Mom hired the woman to take over Ben's responsibilities when it came time for him to head off to college. And he had to admit, the notion of hiring someone in the spring was a good one. With Ben leaving in late summer, the new help would know the ropes for next fall.

But why hire a woman? A woman wouldn't be able to help him in the same way as Ben. A woman would take up another bedroom at the B and B, as well. If Mom had hired a guy, he could have stayed at the farmhouse with Kirk.

Sure, the family owned the old cabin a little more than spitting distance from the B and B. A new hire could stay there, but the place hadn't been cleaned, let alone lived in for years. Neither the electricity or water was turned on. The gal would have to stay at the B and B, which left only two rooms to rent out.

The more Kirk thought about his mom's choice, the more riled he got. He loved his mother, but she often did things with her heart and not her head. He didn't know anything about the woman his mother had found, but he had a strong feeling she would be more of a nuisance than help. Snarling, he gripped the tractor's steering wheel tighter. He'd need to think about a lot of scripture while he worked today if he was going to be even remotely civil with that woman tonight.

Callie Dawson stood to her full height and stretched as far as her five-foot-three-inch body would allow. The pinch in the small of her back had grown to a raging ache. She'd been awarded the prize while carrying box after box of household items into the small cabin. Twisting her body, she kneaded the spot with her right thumb and knuckles. A long, hot soak in a bath would be necessary after she met with the family.

Dread washed over her at the upcoming meeting with Kirk's family. His mother, Tammie, had been more than kind. She was the one who had encouraged Callie to come back. But what would Kirk's dad think? Mike's teasing that she was his second daughter, evening out his children to two boys and two girls, drifted to her mind. She hadn't said goodbye to her "adopted" dad. What about Pamela and Ben, her pretended siblings? What would they think? And Kirk? Her throat tightened and shivers raced down her spine. *What will I say to him?*

Callie released a long breath as she walked into the bathroom and splashed cool water on her face. She wiped off with a towel then peered at her reflection in the mirror. Gripping the sides of the sink, she mumbled, "It's easier to feel nothing. Just don't feel, Callie."

She flopped onto the closed commode, resting her elbows on her knees and cupping her face in her hands. She raked her fingers through her hair then clasped them together. "Who am I kidding? I'm feeling something. I've been 'feeling' the full five years I've been away. It's why I had to get away in the first place." The love she felt for Kirk and his family wrapped around her heart. "It's why I allowed Tammie to talk me into coming back."

She bit the knuckle on her right index finger then stood, staring at her reflection again. "But the feeling doesn't matter. Actions do."

The memory of the day her father walked out on her and her mother resurfaced. Callie and Mom had just returned from a chemo treatment. Her mom's hair had fallen out, all of it, even her eyebrows. Her self-image was shot. Silently a pool of tears filled her eyes. Knowing how sick she was going to be from that day's treatment had weighed on her mother's expression and pulled at Callie's heart.

"You're going to beat this, Mom," Callie said for the millionth time since the initial breast cancer diagnosis, which had been followed by a brief remission, the discovery of new growth, the complete mastectomy, and now chemotherapy and radiation. The clasp to her diamond heart necklace had fallen down her mom's neck, and Callie moved it around to the back. "You'll see. It will be fine."

Her mother hadn't responded, only stared out the windshield. A single tear escaped, and she didn't bother to wipe it away.

Before they got out of the car, Callie's father stepped out of the house, suitcases in both hands. Surprise had wrapped his features when he looked up and saw them sitting in the driveway. They had obviously returned earlier than he'd expected them to. Callie hopped out of the car. "Where you going, Dad?"

He ignored her, heading straight for the truck, which was parked in front of the house. He dropped one suitcase into the bed of the truck, then the other.

"Dad, answer me." Callie grabbed his arm as he made his way to the driver's-side door. She peered back at her mother, who still sat in the passenger's side of the car. Her father brushed her hand away and got into the truck. The window had been rolled down, so she gripped the frame. "Dad?"

Her father stared straight ahead, his expression hard and unfeeling. "I can't do it, Callie."

"Can't do what, Dad?" Fear and anger had swelled within her, spiraling in a way that made her want to throw up and pass out at the same time. The truth of what he planned to do filled her, shredding all respect or affection she'd ever known for the man she'd once called Daddy.

He must have sensed her disdain, because he'd turned to her and for the briefest of moments his face softened and she thought he would get out of the truck and stay with her and her mother. But his expression changed, and he slid the key into the ignition, started the truck and drove away.

A year later, when Callie was only nineteen, her mother lost the battle with cancer. Numb and depressed, Callie meandered through a year working in a clerical position. She and Kirk Jacobs dated. She believed he was on the verge of proposing. She had hoped getting married would alleviate the pain she felt. Then Kirk said he needed a break, and she heard from her dad. Everything changed.

She twirled the diamond heart pendant that hung from her neck, the one her mother had worn for as many years as she could recall. *And Kirk never came for me.*

"Callie Dawson, is that really you?" Kirk's sister, Pamela, hauled open the front door to the B and B.

Callie bit her bottom lip, relief swelling inside her at the twinkle of approval lighting Pamela's eyes. *It's going to be okay. You need to be around people.*

To seal Callie's feeling of relief, a smile bowed Pamela's lips as she grabbed Callie in a hug. "Mom said she hired someone we knew, but I would have never dreamed." She released Callie then nudged her inside. "Come on in. No guests, just family tonight. A perfect time to get reacquainted."

Callie's nerves lifted at Pamela's warm reception. She drank in the sight and smell of the home she'd known so well five years ago. Old-fashioned homey furnishings with touches of Tammie's artistic creations filled the room. The succulent aroma of apple cinnamon mingled perfectly with the decor. The house was just as it had been before and a wave of nostalgia passed through Callie.

"Girls, come meet Callie Dawson," Pamela yelled. She leaned toward Callie. "Course, you've met Emma, but I bet you wouldn't recognize her in a million years."

Within moments, two small red-haired children raced out of the kitchen and stood beside Pamela. "Girls, this is Ms. Callie. She's going to be helping out around the property." Pamela pointed to the slightly taller girl. "Callie, this is Emma."

Callie's eyes widened at the little girl who looked exactly like Pamela, light blue eyes and a splattering of freckles, only Emma had bright red hair. "Pamela, she's gotten so big. She looks just like you."

"I know. Poor thing." Pamela laughed as she pointed to the smaller one. "And this is Emily. We call them Emma and Emmy." Pamela snorted. "If I'd had more sense, I would have given them different names. As you can tell, they look a lot alike and I'm constantly calling out the wrong name."

Callie knelt down in front of the girls. She gawked up at Pamela. "They do look just alike." She tapped Emma's nose with her index finger. "But your hair is a little curlier." Callie turned her attention to Emmy. "And you have your mother's gorgeous dimples."

Deep smiles brightened both their faces. "Do you like to play Candyland?" Emma asked.

"Of course." Callie stood. "When we have time I think that sounds like a lot of fun."

"Yay!" The girls hollered and jumped up and down.

"Uncle Kirk plays with us," Emmy said.

Emma puckered her lip. "When he has time. He's always busy."

Callie's heart flipped at the mention of Kirk. She

decided to change the subject. "Well, Emma, how old are you now?"

Emma grinned anew. "I'm six, and Emmy's five."

"What grade are you in?"

"I'm in kindergarten. Almost to first grade. Momma says I get to start first grade next year."

Emmy pointed to her chest. "And I get to start kindergarten next year."

Emma lifted her chin. "I know how to read."

"I can read a little," said Emmy.

"I bet you're both terrific readers, and I want both of you to read to me some time."

The girls squealed, and Callie stood and crossed her arms in front of her chest. "So, Jack lives here, too? I'm surprised Tammie asked me to help. I mean, with Kirk and Ben and your husband and..."

"Well, Ben is heading to UT in August, and Jack left before Emmy was born. A couple months after you did. I've been a single mom longer than we were together."

"I'm sorry." Guilt niggled her gut. She'd walked out and then Jack followed right behind her. *Well, I didn't exactly walk out. It was Kirk who wanted a break, and who would have known that Dad—*

"Don't be." Pamela's words interrupted her thoughts. "He kept getting worse..."

Before Pamela could finish, Ben walked into the room, and Callie's mouth dropped. When she'd left, Ben had been an awkward teenager who still had a lot of growing to do. Now, the boy towered several inches taller and sported the same dark shadows on his chin that Kirk always had at the end of the day. If Callie didn't know better, she would have mistaken him for Kirk.

"Hey, Callie." Ben scooped her up in his arms and

twirled her around, squeezing the breath out of her. "Bet you never thought I'd be able to do that." Mischief twinkled in his eyes when he put her back on her feet.

"Ben, I can't believe it's you."

"We've missed you."

A knot formed in her throat, and she swallowed back the regret and sadness that overpowered her. Ben had always been the straight shooter in the family. He didn't mince words, and he didn't mind expressing how he saw things or how he felt. She envied that about him.

Kirk had never come for her, but she'd still been like part of this family. She shouldn't have allowed her circumstances to keep her from talking with them. "I missed you all, too." Emotion threatened to overwhelm her and she smiled. "More than I even realized." She punched Ben's arm. "But look at you, all grown up."

He straightened his shoulders and lifted his chin. "I'm quite handsome, aren't I?"

Callie laughed out loud. "And, still just like the Ben I remember."

"I think I recognize that laugh." A deep voice sounded from the top of the stairs. In a flash, Kirk's dad, Mike, descended the stairs with Tammie following. Callie was awarded two more hugs. Mike kissed the top of her head. "It's good to see you, girl. Tammie told me you were coming to stay with us. What a blessing."

"I think it's me receiving the blessing." Callie smiled up at him, a peace and acceptance she hadn't felt in a long time welled within her. How many nights had she spent caring for a dying mother and then a dying father and then dying patients? Death had surrounded her for so many years; she had forgotten what life was like.

Being in this home for only a few minutes and she was already beginning to remember. And it felt oh, so good.

The front door opened then slammed shut. Callie sucked in her breath. The two girls jumped on the grizzly of a man who walked in. "Uncle Kirk!" They shouted in unison. He welcomed their attention, wrapping them both in a bear hug at one time. Placing them back on their feet, he looked up, his eyes widening when he saw Callie.

Shivers raced down Callie's spine and her hands started to shake at the sight of the only man she'd ever loved. Her body's reaction stunned her, but she forced a hesitant smile. "Hi, Kirk."

Surprise erased from his expression as he furrowed his brow and scowled. "I thought you were dead."

Chapter 2

A nervous giggle slipped through Callie's lips as she patted her arms and legs. "Nope. Not dead. I'm as alive as I've ever been."

Kirk's expression didn't change as his gaze shifted from her to his family. Callie didn't have to look at the others. The tension in the room was thick as death, and she knew they also were bewildered by his comment.

"I told you to stop saying that." Pamela slipped the words through gritted teeth.

Callie gawked at her friend. Was that something he said often? Maybe they weren't bewildered. Maybe just stunned that she was alive. Why would they think she was dead?

Remorse filled her anew because she hadn't contacted Kirk when she made it to her dad's house in Jackson, Tennessee. Confusion replaced her regret. *But wouldn't he be glad to see me, hugging me even, if he thought I'd died and then discovered I was still alive?*

She gazed back at the man who, five years ago, she would have been willing to spend the rest of her life with if things had been different. The fury raging in his eyes was proof enough he'd never believed her dead. Only dead to him.

Aggravated, Callie lifted her shoulders and chin. The overgrown bully would not intimidate her. In her experience, bullies ran away when confronted, and Kirk Jacobs was about to be just that. "Did you hear on the news that I had died?" Callie's tone dripped with sarcasm as she crossed her arms in front of her chest, bracing herself for a verbal battle. "Did you attend my funeral?"

Kirk mimicked her stance. "No, but we sure heard you got married."

Callie gasped, then a loud clap sounded. She turned toward the maker of the interruption.

"Well, it's about time for me to head over to the house." Ben nodded his head toward Callie. He clicked his tongue and winked, reminding her of the boy she remembered. "See ya tomorrow, Cals," he said as he sprinted out the back entrance.

"Yeah, and the girls and I need to run to the store." Pamela grabbed her purse and motioned for her children.

"But I don't want to go to the store." Emmy stomped her foot and stuck out her lip. "I haven't seen Uncle Kirk in forever."

"Yeah." Emma joined in, twirling a red curl between her fingertips. "He promised to play Candyland with us."

"No sassing." Pamela scooped up two pairs of sandals from beside the back door and handed them to the children. "Put these on."

"I can't do the buckles," Emmy whined and threw her pair onto the floor.

"These aren't mine, Mom," Emma snapped and let hers fall, as well. "You gave me the wrong pair."

"Looks like you're going to need a little help," Tammie responded before Pamela could scold the children. She peered down at her granddaughters. "Do we talk to our mother that way?"

Both girls' chins dropped. "Sorry, Mommy."

"That's better." Pamela waited while the girls flopped onto the floor to put on their shoes. "We've no time for that."

Tammie added, "Just pick them up. We'll put them on in the car." She turned to her husband, and Callie was struck again at how little Tammie had aged in five years. Choppy, shoulder-length dark hair and bright green eyes, the woman looked nothing like any grandma Callie had ever known. "Mike, you need to check on the…on the…"

Mike snapped his fingers. "On the horses." Though Callie and Mike had shared nothing more than a quick hug since her return, she still saw the same quiet kindness behind his deep gray eyes.

"Yes." Tammie grabbed his elbow then waved at Callie with her free hand. "We'll see you tomorrow, Callie."

Callie couldn't believe so many people had cleared the room so fast. She frowned at Kirk and shook her head. "I'm sorry, Kirk. Did you just say I was married?"

"That's right." Kirk walked across the room and plopped down in a large brown recliner. "So, where is Mr. High and Mighty?"

"I never got married."

He leaned back. "Sure, you did. Pamela heard it straight from the guy's mouth."

Callie rubbed her temple with the tips of her fingers. For the life of her, she had no idea what Kirk was talking about. She hadn't even gone on a date with anyone except Kirk. No one had even asked—well, that wasn't exactly true. There was a hospice patient in his late sixties who she'd grown quite fond of, and he had always said if he were forty years younger and in good health, he would have snatched her up.

Callie's stomach turned. Frank's death seemed to forge the final crack in Callie's already-breaking heart. But Callie felt pretty sure Kirk wasn't talking about the elderly hospice patient. "What guy? I've never been married."

"That dark-haired fellow you left with. The one who drove the red Corvette. Gotta admit it. Though I didn't like the guy much, he sure had good taste in vehicles."

Callie furrowed her eyebrows. "You mean Bill?"

Kirk shrugged. "I didn't know his name. He told Pamela at the store that you two were getting hitched."

Callie tried to wrap her mind around the information and how it could have possibly gotten so distorted. She made her way to the couch across from Kirk and plopped down. "Bill is my cousin, my dad's brother's son. I'd never even met him until the week he showed up here. Evidently, my dad and his dad had a serious falling out when they were teenagers and never spoke to each other until..."

Callie let the sentence drop. She didn't want to revisit everything again. She'd spent the past three years trying to recover by throwing every piece of herself into the encouragement and aid of others. She finally realized nursing terminal patients was not the place for her to be. *At least not right now. Not until I'm healed.*

Kirk frowned and for a brief moment Callie saw a glimmer of hope, or maybe even affection, behind his gaze. Callie steeled herself to the slight jolt to her heart. She didn't need to think about Kirk. She needed…

Kirk's words interrupted her thoughts. "But he said…"

"Bill was getting married the very next Saturday after he came here to get me, but he wasn't marrying me."

"But Pamela said…"

Callie shook her head. "Pamela must have misunderstood. I've never married."

"But you left."

"I had to."

"Why?"

"Why does it matter? You broke it off with me, remember?" Callie smacked her hands against the couch. "Kirk, you hadn't spoken to me for two months before I left." She lifted her pointer and middle fingers. "Two months. You said you needed a break."

Kirk rubbed his hands together. "I didn't mean it."

"Two months of nothing, Kirk. I think that shows you meant it."

The memory of that time would be forever marked in his mind. As his feelings for Callie had grown stronger, so had his fear of commitment. He'd fallen in love with her, and the admission of it, even if only to himself, terrified him. The first few days after the suggested break, Kirk threw himself into farm work. By the end of the first week things started going wrong on the farm—a calf born breech, a fallen tree that tore down part of the fence. One mishap after another kept him from getting in touch with Callie and asking her to forgive his foolishness. Two months later, Bill showed up. Then pride wouldn't allow Kirk to contact her.

And he let her go. Just like that.

He'd been a fool. He stood and walked away from her penetrating gaze. Callie followed behind him. She grabbed his arm and turned him until he had no choice but to gaze down into her crystal-blue eyes. Honesty and sincerity radiated from the orbs, twisting his heart.

"You never came for me."

"I thought you got married." His words came out in a whisper. They didn't sound convincing even to his own ears.

"But you never even confronted me about that. We dated all those years and you thought I would up and marry a guy after two months apart?"

Her words cut at him, and he winced at the pain as he looked away from her gaze. What had he been thinking? A man who loved his woman would chase the guy down and show him with his fists who had the right to his girl's hand. But, Kirk had carried too much pride to go after her. He'd always been too proud, too worried about someone getting the best of him. It was something God had worked with him on for the past several years. "You still left. Why?"

Callie closed her eyes. "It's a long story."

"I'm listening."

Callie opened her eyes and shook her head. "No. Not tonight." She exhaled a long breath. "I think I need to head over to the cabin for tonight."

Kirk frowned. "No. You'll stay here. The cabin's a mess. No electricity. No water. No—"

"It's all ready and fixed up for me. Tammie and Mike worked on it all week."

Kirk hadn't noticed his parents working on the cabin. But then they would have wanted to keep Callie's upcoming appearance from him. Still, he would have helped. It upset him to think his family would keep such a big task from him. "At least let me walk you over there."

Callie shook her head. "No, really, Kirk. I need some time alone."

She turned and walked out the door. It had been a long while since Kirk felt so low. He'd been wrong in more ways tonight...and in the past five years...than he was able to count. Pride, which almost always reared its ugly head in the form of ranting anger, had once again bested him. And once again, he'd embarrassed himself in front of the people he cared about most. "Forgive me, Lord."

Callie awakened at dawn to a rooster's crows and a dog's bark, and the noises had never before sounded more glorious. After five years of cars and trains, Callie welcomed the much earlier rising time if it included such wonderful accompaniment. The ability to inhale fresh, clean air wasn't too bad, either. Pushing the night before and its verbal exchange with Kirk as far back in her mind as possible, Callie stared up at the ceiling. "God, I could so get used to this again."

With a nudging of excitement welling in her spirit, Callie slipped out of the covers and put on her fluffy multicolored socks and fuzzy, hot-pink robe. As soon as she brewed a good, strong cup of coffee, she would head over to the barn to see the animals. Too many years had slipped by since she'd spent time with nature, and her senses were long overdue.

The sunrise caught her attention through the small kitchen window. Racing to the back door, Callie flung it open and sucked in the majesty of God's creation. The huge white-gold sphere seemed to rise from the ground as it pushed its way through waves of red, orange and yellow. The earth screamed the arrival of a new day, and Callie bit back her tears. *Oh, God, I needed this. I needed to see life, to see Your awesome majesty.*

Hurrying around the kitchen, Callie made her coffee, adding sugar and cream just the way she liked it. She slipped on a T-shirt and jeans and a pair of rubber boots, rushed out the back door and headed toward the barn. Newly grown grass crunched ever so slightly beneath her feet. Dandelions carpeted the ground, but even they reminded her of the rebirth of spring.

Without thinking, she bent down and plucked several from the earth. She stuck one behind her ear, then twisted the stems of several more together until they were long enough to drape her neck as a necklace. "How many years has it been since I wore one of these?"

She giggled as she continued her trek to the barn. No one would be there at this time. Kirk and Ben would have already done their chores close to home and would be out in the fields by now. At least, she hoped so. Even the chance of running into Kirk couldn't sway her from seeing the animals.

The memory of their argument made her almost laugh out loud. *The big goof thought I was married.* The knowledge of what she had been doing those five years swept over her. *I would have rather been married than...*

She bent down and plucked another dandelion. *I will*

not think about that, Lord. Help me focus on You and the wonder of Your creation.

Excitement welled in her chest as she passed several trees budding with flowers, thinking of the fruit that would soon appear. She paused at the chicken coop, laughing at the baby chicks fighting for food. Finally, she made her way to the barn, hoping upon hope the mare she'd cherished would still be there. Her heart sank at the empty stall, even though she knew the horse might be in the field.

"Looking for someone?"

Callie jumped at the sound of Ben's voice behind her. She turned and saw the young man standing beside her beloved brown mare. Callie walked over and caressed the white patch on the horse's nose. "Princess."

"She's not as strong as she used to be." Ben rubbed the side of her neck. "Broke her leg about four years back."

Callie gasped, covering her mouth with her hand. "Oh, no."

Ben nodded. "The vet suggested we put her down. But Kirk wouldn't let her go."

Callie noticed a shadow to her left. She looked and saw Kirk watching them. His gaze seemed haunted, and thick wrinkles around his eyes spoke of a sleepless night. For all his gruffness, Callie knew he'd been blindsided to find out she'd never married. She knew he was proud, but why would he be willing to save her horse, but let her go?

Chapter 3

Kirk walked to the B and B while Ben and Callie got the petting zoo ready for the school group scheduled to arrive later that day. He knew Mom and Pamela would be busy getting treats ready for the kids, but he needed to talk with his sister. He pushed open the door with a huff and marched over to Pamela. "She never married."

"Uncle Kirk," Emmy squealed.

"Not now," Pamela scolded, and Emmy's expression fell.

Kirk's heart softened at the sight of his niece. "Go set up the game in the dining room. I'll be in there in a minute."

Kirk rumpled Emmy's hair, then looked back at his sister. He shrugged at her grin and raised eyebrow. "What? A man can take a minute's break for his niece. The game won't take long, especially since Emma's at school and it will just be the two of us."

He hardened his expression, crossing his arms in front of his chest. "But you and I both know that's not why I've come."

Pamela stopped rinsing the strawberries and wiped her hands on a towel. "Kirk, the man said plain as day that he was marrying Callie."

Kirk squinted his eyes. "What were his words exactly?"

"Come on, Kirk." Pamela brushed a strand of hair out of her eyes with the back of her hand. "That was five years ago, but it was something like, 'Next Saturday I'm marrying Callie.'"

"Actually, he married a lady named Allie."

Pamela frowned. "Allie?"

"Yeah. I looked them up on the internet."

"You looked them up?"

Noting the humor in his mother's voice, he turned toward her. "What? You can find out anything on the internet."

"Yeah, but—" His mom laughed.

Pamela joined her. "Who would have ever thought you would actually do it."

Kirk squinted and pursed his lips. His mom cut the top off a strawberry then glanced up at Kirk. "Okay. So, it was a simple misunderstanding."

"A simple misunderstanding!" Kirk boomed. He glared at Pamela. "I hardly think losing Callie can be labeled a misunderstanding."

Pamela shrank beneath his outburst, and Kirk cringed. His sister had lived with the fury of an irrational man, one who rarely treated her as he should. She and Jack never divorced, but as long as he continued to tip the bottle, Kirk was glad the guy stayed away. He would even make sure the guy stayed away if the need arose. He took a long, deep breath. "I'm sorry, Pamela."

She shrugged her shoulders as his mother placed the paring knife on the counter with a loud tap. "Son, you're the one who didn't seek out Callie to find the truth."

"I know, Mom." Kirk had punished himself all night for his foolishness. He wished he would have swallowed his pride, found her and convinced her to stay with him.

"I'm so mad at myself." His mother picked the knife up again and snapped off two strawberry tops in one swipe. "That girl's been through a lot. I knew she didn't have a mother to help her." Her hands shook as desperately as her voice. "I should have gone after her. What kind of Christian woman…"

"Mom." A knot formed in Kirk's throat as he wrapped one arm around his mother and the other around Pamela. Concern for them and Callie nearly took his breath away as he held them and a slight sniffle sounded from his mother. He swallowed back the knot in his throat. "Mom, what did she go through? Why did she leave?"

His mother moved out of his embrace, grabbed a tissue and dotted her eyes. She peered up at Kirk. "Son, I don't know." She shook her head and looked out the kitchen window. "A couple weeks ago, I met her while she was kneeling in front of her mother's grave. When she looked up at me, I saw a deep-to-the-core sadness." She tapped her chest as she gazed back at Kirk. "And, I knew in my spirit that God wanted us to help her."

Kirk scratched his chin with his finger and thumb. "But what did she say?"

Mom shook her head. "She didn't *say* anything. She didn't want to talk about it. Oh, she said a few things, like having to work really hard when she left, but I have no idea what the girl has really been doing these last five years."

Kirk thought a moment. "She did say that Bill was her dad's nephew, and that she'd never met him before that week."

"Maybe she reunited with her dad," Pamela said.

His mother put down her strawberry and knife once again, wiped off her hands then touched Pamela and Kirk's arms. "I'm telling you, it doesn't matter what's happened in the past. She'll let us know all that when the time is right. What she needs right now is for us to love on her a bit."

Kirk pursed his lips and nodded. Loving her wouldn't be an issue. He'd never stopped loving her. Trusting her, being around her day after day, being willing to be hurt by her again—now those things might be a bit of a problem.

Callie had promised God and herself that when she returned to Bloom Hollow she would read scripture, even if only a little bit, every morning. In her excitement at the sunrise and the promise of seeing the animals, she had forgotten and now it was almost time for the school group to visit. She didn't have time to race back to the cabin now. *God, I'm sorry. You've given me this new start, and I want my focus to be on You.*

Her mind traveled to the inspiring sunrise she'd witnessed that morning. Her thoughts and heart had been lifted in praise at His majesty and she knew her spirit encouraged her, and that she had worshipped Him and was forgiven.

"I can hardly wait for the children to come," Callie

said to Ben as she allowed the goat to eat a bit of food from her palm.

"Not me," Ben huffed. "The kids drive me crazy. They climb on the fences, pull at the animals. They scream and yell and make a big mess." He pointed at his chest. "A mess that little brother Ben always seems to get assigned to clean up."

Callie laughed.

Ben waggled his eyebrows. "Hey, but you're the new Ben. Maybe, I'll pass that job on to you."

Callie placed her hand over her heart. "I would be honored to have the job of cleaning up after the kiddos. It will be a wonderful change from what I've been doing."

"What have you been doing?"

"Stuff that is a lot worse."

"Really?"

"And dirtier." Callie paused and sucked in a deep breath. "And harder."

Ben seemed to understand her need to change the subject because he grabbed her shoulders, gave her a little shake then rubbed the top of her head with his knuckles, forming a rat's nest on the top of her head. "Then it's official. Callie gets to clean up."

She swatted his hand then raked her fingers through her hair. "You big goob."

He shrugged away, laughing. Callie knew, without a doubt, God had called her back to Bloom Hollow, Tennessee. And it felt good to be home.

Kirk watched Callie as she led the small group of children around the petting zoo. The group was one of the smaller ones, only two grades from the local elementary school. It was a great start for Callie. She stopped in front of the goat. One of the smaller boys walked up to old Tom and tried to kick his back leg while an older girl tried to pet his nose, but Callie kept control of the situation by scooping up the youngster in one arm and helping the girl with the other. Old Tom was saved from mistreatment.

"Let's head over to the sheep." Callie's voice carried through the air. A smile never left her face as she guided a timid girl in petting the animal.

Finished with the animals, Callie guided the group to the playground area constructed several years before by Kirk, his brother and his dad. He grinned as she slid down the curving slide with the rascal of a boy who tried to kick the goat. The little guy then led her to the seesaw, and on to the merry-go-round.

"Will you play with me, Uncle Kirk?" He looked down at the big, doe-like eyes of his younger niece.

"Sure, Emmy. Just lead the way."

She clapped her hands and headed straight for the merry-go-round. "Uncle Kirk will push us," she hollered.

Surprise and a twinge of pink dotted Callie's cheeks as she got off the merry-go-round and swiped at her pant legs.

"No, stay with me, Miss Callie," the little guy yelled.

Kirk motioned to an empty spot on the ride. "If you don't hurry, you'll lose it."

Callie sat and wrapped one arm around the bar and the other around the little boy. Kirk relished the pure pleasure that marked her face as he pushed the ride.

"I think I'm gonna get sick," the boy moaned as he nodded his head back and forth, up and down.

Kirk stopped the merry-go-round, hoping to get the

kid off before he threw up all over the place. A hacking sound escaped his lips and he vomited all over Callie's shirt and pants. As good-natured as she'd always been, Callie shrugged and laughed as she handed the kid over to a chaperone. "I'll be right back."

"I'm so sorry," the chaperone said as she pulled tissues from her purse, handing some to Callie and wiping off the child at the same time.

"No, really." She handed the tissues back to the woman and pointed to the cabin. "I live over there. I can go clean up quickly." She looked up at Kirk, her gaze darting from him to the chaperone.

Kirk snapped back to the present. "You can take him to the B and B. My mother can get you some towels to clean him up."

"Thanks." The woman seemed overwhelmed as she and the boy headed to the house. Callie started toward the cabin when Ben raced over to her. "Told you it was messy."

Kirk chuckled as she acted as if she were going to give Ben a hug and he ran away.

A long sigh escaped his lips. He'd have never dreamed it would feel so nice to see Callie on the farm again. He hadn't given himself time to take it in when he first saw her, but Callie had changed.

She still had her long, flowing blond hair and her crystal-blue eyes. Beautiful as ever. And she was still a small slip of a woman, but she was just that—a woman. Her father's desertion and her mother's death had taken a lot out of her all those years ago, but his mom was right, more had happened. She was calm and happy as she'd been before, but Kirk noted she was reserved, as well, almost as if a wall separated her from other people.

"Oh, no, where's Timmy?" The frustrated sound of the same chaperone, laced with a bit of fear, broke Kirk from his thoughts.

"He's not on the playground?"

The woman scanned the area again. "I cleaned him up and told him he could come back here while I washed my hands." She bit her bottom lip. "But I don't see him."

"He couldn't have gone far."

"You don't know Timmy."

A quick sense of dread washed over him at the woman's words. He glanced from the petting area to the B and B and around the expanse of the yard. "Ben, we've got a kiddo missing."

"On it." Ben raced toward the barn to be sure the little rascal hadn't wandered in there. Kirk headed toward the house.

"Kirk, come quick!" Tammie yelled.

Kirk ran to the fence behind the B and B and the cabin. The boy who'd vomited on Callie lay on the ground with a huge, bleeding gash on his right arm below his elbow. His face had paled as tears streamed down his cheeks.

The chaperone reached them a moment after Kirk. She covered her mouth with her hand. "I can't do blood." Without another word, the woman collapsed to the ground, making the boy sob harder.

"Here, I got him." A cleaned-up Callie now stood behind him. "Make sure the woman is okay."

Shocked, Kirk stood still while his mother helped the lady and Callie took over with the boy.

"Okay, Timmy, Miss Callie's going to make it all better." She plopped a bag beside him and pulled out cotton and antiseptic wipes to clean the wound.

"Looks like he'll need stitches," Tammie said as she soothed the boy's mom.

"Oh," the woman moaned as if about to vomit, while the boy wailed at the top of his lungs.

"I think I can butterfly it." Callie pulled strips out of the bag. "Kirk, could you hold Timmy from behind? That may make him feel better."

Callie wiped Timmy's brow and cheek with the back of her hand while Kirk sat behind the boy. "There now, Timmy. It will be all right."

Kirk gently maneuvered the boy into his lap while Callie finished dressing his cut. He was surprised at the ease with which Callie worked, as if she'd done it many times before. His curiosity piqued.

"Looks like we got a few splinters to deal with, as well." Callie pointed to the child's right hand.

Kirk bit back a gasp. No less than fifty small slivers of wood had pierced the boy's hand. "How in the world?" Kirk glanced behind him. The boy must have tried to climb the barbed-wire fence by supporting himself against the wooden post. He shook his head. Well, the boy wouldn't try climbing barbed wire again.

"You ready?" Callie nodded at Kirk. She held a pair of tweezers in her hand.

"Sure."

"Okay. Here we go."

For the next hour or more, Kirk watched as Callie patiently and meticulously removed one splinter after another. Every once in a while Timmy whimpered and Callie soothed him with calming words and tones. Kirk had never seen her so confident, so self-assured, so capable.

Again, he watched the change in Callie. Despite her

mutterings of tenderness to the child, he felt her disconnect from true emotion. Though she might resist, he intended to find out what had happened to her. Her body returned to Bloom Hollow, but Callie was still missing. He intended to find her. And this time, he wasn't going to let her go.

Chapter 4

Callie nudged Ben's arm as they walked into the house for dinner. "What was that you said about the new help having to clean up after the kiddos?"

Ben blew out an exaggerated breath. "It ain't right. Even after Mom hires some help, I still get stuck cleaning up paper cups and napkins, chewed gum and candy wrappers, wiping down play equipment and taking out trash." He threw up his hands. "I don't know what a guy's gotta do to move out of custodial services in this joint."

Callie laughed. Out of the corner of her eye, she saw Tammie shaking her head at her dramatic son. Callie lifted one eyebrow and squinted. "I'd have been happy to switch jobs. You could have picked out splinters for an hour and a half, cleaned blood—"

Ben raised his hands. "Oh, no. Those jobs can be left

to you. I'd have been lying on the ground beside that boy's chaperone if I'd had to take care of him."

Mike patted his son's shoulders. "Truer words have never been spoken."

Kirk walked through the back screen door and took off his ball cap. Callie's heartbeat sped up at the sight of his disheveled hat head. In the past, she'd have teased him while she ruffled some life back into his hair. "Makes no sense to me. The boy can birth a calf or mend any kind of wound on an animal without blinking an eye, but a person—"

"Can't take no people blood," said Ben as he sat at the table.

Tammie clicked her tongue. "That's enough talk about injuries. Let's eat before the food gets cold."

The family sat, and Callie noticed they'd left the same chair she used to sit in open for her. Nostalgia washed over her as she slipped into the seat. Swallowing back her emotions, she bowed her head while Mike offered a quick prayer. Emma chattered about her kindergarten class while the family passed the large bowls of mixed salad, baked spaghetti and garlic bread. It was one of her favorite meals, and Callie knew Tammie had fixed it for her.

Thankful for Emma's ramblings, Callie sucked in a deep breath. Years had passed since she'd felt part of a family. She tried to remember the last time someone had fixed a dinner for her. Probably at this very house. She studied her plate, afraid to look up. This was what she wanted. What she'd dreamed for. Even though she hadn't realized how much she longed for it. Family. Home. Her chest swelled. It was almost too much.

"What's for dessert, Mom?"

She grinned as she looked up and saw Mike tap Tammie's hand. She'd always thought it cute how they called each other "Mom" and "Dad."

"Pamela's homemade strawberry pie."

Callie sighed along with the family's mumblings of approval. Pamela's strawberry pie was melt-in-your-mouth good. A perfect blend of sweet and tart with crust so flaky a girl couldn't help but lick her finger and press it to the plate to be sure to get every last crumb.

Taking another bite of her salad, Callie smiled as she watched the family interact. Ben and Mike discussed something about one of the animals, while Pamela prompted Emmy to eat more of her spaghetti and Emma continued to share every detail about her day with Tammie. Callie swallowed the bite as she realized Kirk's gaze was locked on her.

"So, where'd you learn to fix people up like that, Cals?"

Hearing Ben use her nickname was one thing, but coming from Kirk's lips was something altogether different. She clasped her hands under the table as she looked at Kirk. His gaze held questions. More than she wanted to answer, at least right now. "I didn't do anything that great. Just taped up a cut and pulled out a few splinters."

She realized the chatter had ceased around the table and all attention stayed on her. She lowered her gaze to her plate then took a bite of spaghetti, hoping they'd go back to their conversations.

"No. I'd say it was a bit more than that."

Callie glanced back at Kirk. Picking up her napkin, she dabbed her mouth. She knew him. He wasn't going to let it go. "Well, I have worked as a nurse for a few years."

"You got your nursing degree?"

Callie looked at Pamela and remembered her longing to go to school, but Jack had been unstable and Emma had come along so quickly. A pang of sorrow washed over her for Kirk's sister. "It's not easy when you're trying to take care of family, but it can be done. I promise. I—"

"You say that like you know what it's like."

Callie focused on Kirk again. She'd almost said more than she wanted. She didn't want to talk about her dad. Sure, the family would gush over her. They'd say they understood and be sweet and kind. But she wasn't ready for all that. Didn't want pity. She wanted closure. To move on with her life.

Determined not to comment, she took a swallow of the sweet tea then stabbed her salad again.

"What kind of nursing did you do? Work in a hospital? A doctor's office?" asked Mike.

Callie stared at her plate. "Actually, I worked for hospice. I traveled to the homes of patients and made them comfortable before they died."

Pamela gasped. Callie knew it sounded morbid. To a degree, it was very morbid. But a part of her had been thankful to help people in their last days and hours. To give them peace. Show them love. But she'd slipped away from her relationship with God, and after a few years, death had become her existence. Had robbed her of joy.

Tammie rested her hand on top of Callie's. "Those people were blessed to have you, Callie. You're one of the kindest people I know."

Callie nodded as she thought of her last patient. She missed Frank's sweet smile and kind heart. He never failed to make her day when she stopped by to check his vitals and give him medicine. Despite his chronic pain from congestive heart failure and emphysema, he made sure to tell her she was beautiful, that he wanted nothing more than to sweep her off her feet. His faith had been a light to her. When he died, it was as if all the light in her life went out. She knew she needed to find God again.

"What about that Bill? Your father's nephew. Why did he come to Bloom Hollow?"

Kirk's question brought Callie back to the present. She pushed away from the table. She wasn't ready to go there. Not to Bill, his dad or her father. Not now, anyway. "I'm feeling really tired. Haven't recovered from traveling, I suppose. I think I'm going to head on over to the cabin."

"What about pie?" asked Emma. "It's so good."

Callie smiled at the sweet urchin. "Make sure they save me a piece, okay?"

Emma nodded, and Callie excused herself and walked out the screen door.

"Give her a little time, son. She'll talk to us when she's ready."

Mike's voice followed her across the porch. She wished Kirk would listen to his father, though she figured he wouldn't. For five years he was willing to pretend she was dead. Now he wanted to know all that had happened in the time she'd been gone. But Kirk Jacobs had given up any rights to know anything about her life since he'd decided to kill her off in his mind. He should have gone after her.

* * *

"Kirk, you're only going to make things worse. She needs time."

Kirk shrugged away from his mother's hold on his arm. "You've invited her back into our home, into our lives. The least she can do is tell us what sent her skipping out of town."

His mother narrowed her gaze and planted both hands on her hips. "I didn't ask with strings attached, son." She pointed toward the cabin. "If you have eyes at all, you can tell she's had a rough go-around. She needs some time. She'll open it—"

"I'm tired of y'all telling me to give her space. She's been here a week. She's had space. She left us—" he extended his arm to include everyone at the table "—all of us, high and dry, without an explanation of any kind. No goodbyes. She just left." Done with talking, he pushed through the screen door.

"Thing aren't always as simple as they appear, Kirk."

He jumped off the back porch then turned and peered up at his mother. "You shouldn't have hired her without asking the rest of us. You're not the only one throwing your whole life into this land."

Without a backward glance, Kirk stomped to the old cabin. Conviction niggled at his heart, and he knew when he left Callie, he'd have to head back to the main house to give his mom a whopping of an apology. He forged ahead. Right now, he couldn't think about that. He needed to find out why Callie left and why she never once contacted him.

In one motion, he hopped onto the small deck and pushed open the front door. Callie gasped, and Kirk realized she'd released her long, straight blond locks from their knot. The mass of her hair drifted past her left shoulder, and the memory of its full softness washed over him. Fury filled her gaze and she pointed to the door. "Get out, Kirk."

He planted his feet on the hardwood and crossed his arms in front of his chest. "No."

"You have no right to walk into someone's house, and—"

"This is my house. I pay the taxes on it. I take care of it."

His gaze took in the shiny hardwood floors, the whitewashed walls and the blue curtains. The furnishings were sparse, a blue-and-white checkered couch, a blue wingback chair, a simple wood table with two chairs, but it was cleaner than he'd seen it in years. His parents had done a great job preparing it for Callie. Above the table, he spied the painting of a young woman and a horse. Callie'd had that picture for as long as he knew her. He wasn't sure why she liked it so much. It really wasn't all that pretty.

She stepped toward him until her small frame was only inches from his. Her hands were drawn into fists at her sides as she speared him with a look of utter contempt. "I am paying for this cabin by the work I am doing on this farm, and I am telling you to leave my home."

"No. Not until you tell me why you left. You owe me that."

"I owe you nothing. You broke it off, remember? We weren't dating. You had spoken maybe five words to me in two months."

Kirk swallowed. He hated himself for that. She couldn't fathom how many nights he'd beat himself to a pulp over his stupidity. She was all he'd ever wanted, and he'd let her go. "What about my family? You didn't even say goodbye to them."

Pain flashed across her features, and Kirk strengthened his resolve. He had her there. "That was wrong of me. I wish I could change that."

There she was, the Callie he knew and loved. The one who cared about his family. She hadn't admitted to caring about him, but surely she did. He couldn't possibly have been alone in how much he loved her.

He started to uncross his arms. If he wrapped her up in a hug, she'd settle down. All would be well. She'd forgive him for breaking up with her, tell him what happened and he'd forgive her for leaving.

She poked his chest with her finger. "Get out of my home, Kirk."

"Why did you leave?"

"It's none of your business."

"Of course it's my business. Tell me why. Where did you go? Who were you with? I can forgive you and we can move on if you'll just tell me—"

"You can forgive me!" Callie walked away from him and grabbed her cell phone off the table. "I'm giving you five seconds to leave this cabin before I call the police."

"Now, Callie."

"Kirk, I have papers, drawn up and legal, which say I'm paying to live here. You can leave the easy way or the hard way."

"I just want you to tell me what happened. You owe—"

"For the last time, I owe you nothing." She pointed to the door. "Get out."

Anger and frustration warred within him as he

stomped out of the house. Why was she being so difficult? Was she hiding something? Another guy? *God, all she has to do is tell me what happened. I don't think I'm asking so much. We dated all through high school. She's the only woman I've loved. Why is caring about where she's been so wrong?*

God seemed quiet as he made his way to the small house he shared with his brother. By the time he'd reached the porch, he realized that his dad rocked in the chair out front. He stood to his full height, and Kirk knew twenty-five years from now he'd be the spitting image of the man. Salt-and-pepper hair, worn skin from hours in the sun, but a strong back and working hands. "I reckon you and I need to walk on back to the main house together."

Guilt resurfaced in the pit of his gut. He knew what his dad wanted. An apology for his mom. Kirk nodded. "I imagine you're right."

His dad stepped of the porch and wrapped his arm around Kirk's shoulder. "Your mom will forgive you, but I don't ever want to hear you speak like that to her again."

"Yes, sir."

Kirk followed his dad back to the house. A few yards away, his dad stopped and turned toward Kirk. "I know you want Callie to open up to you. But it really does take time, son. Remember when we first got Thunder?"

Kirk thought of the day they'd received the horse. He'd been abused, and as a result was angry and feisty, and it took time, a lot of time, to break him. Kirk nodded.

"I'm not saying Callie's been abused. I don't know

what happened to her. But she's hurting. And it's going to take time and a gentle hand to win her over."

Kirk thought of days he'd spent wooing Thunder to trust him, the nights he'd ask God for guidance because in his gut he knew Thunder would one day be a great horse. He'd had such patience with Thunder. Shown him so much love. He could do the same for Callie.

Chapter 5

Two weeks had passed since Callie threw him out of the cabin. School would be out for the summer in less than two weeks, which would decrease the traffic on the playground area and the petting zoo. But warmer temperatures had already arrived causing a consistent influx of customers for the bed-and-breakfast and their small lunch café. With farm chores to add to everything, he'd had no time to talk with Callie again. Course, it seemed to him she'd been avoiding him, anyway.

He pulled his prized black Ford F150 into the hardware store parking lot and turned off the engine. The tractor had broken down again. He planned to look at a few new ones after buying what he needed to fix Old Bertha. He'd have to twist his dad's arm when it came time to get rid of the tractor for good. The old girl had been working the farm since before Kirk was born. But the time had nearly come for her to go to pasture in a junkyard somewhere. A man couldn't spend two days of his week fixing antique farm equipment.

The tractor might have even been the reason he hadn't been able to spend any time with Callie. She'd proven to be a great help to his mom and sister. And she didn't seem to mind lending a hand with farm chores, even mending equipment, which he'd never been able to get Pamela to do. Still, when it came time to help, she stayed close to his dad or Ben. Against his will, he'd stayed close to Old Bertha.

He walked to the front of the store. Before he could grab the handle, the door opened and an old high school friend walked out. "Hey Kirk, how's it going?"

Kirk shook Zack's hand. "Good. How 'bout you?"

He pointed toward the shop. "Greta's got me building her a gazebo for the backyard. I came out to load the truck up with the wood while she paid. Not sure I want to know the damage."

"I understand."

"Hey, I hear Callie's back in town."

Kirk nodded. "She is. Working with us on the farm."

"You two getting back together?"

Heat raced up Kirk's neck and cheeks. Part of him wanted to say they were. The other part wanted to kick her back to wherever she'd been the past several years. He still loved her. No doubt about that. But she sure didn't want anything to do with him, and having her around was like running through barbed wire each and every time he saw her.

Before he could answer, the door opened again, and Greta and her younger sister, Heather, walked out. A blush reddened Heather's cheeks when she looked up at him. He knew she had a crush on him. Had for years.

She was a bit homely. No sense trying to say it any other way, but she was as nice a girl as they came.

He nodded toward them. "Afternoon, ladies. Zack says you got him building you a gazebo, Greta."

"Yeah. It will be nice to have to watch the birds and butterflies and all, but I thought it would also be a nice place for family and friends to sit and eat when we have a cookout."

Kirk nodded. "Zack, I'll have to come by and see how it looks when you get done. Might be something Mom would like to have."

"Of course you should come by, Kirk." Greta nudged Heather closer to him, and he watched as her face flushed even redder. "You could come for a cookout. I know your mom and sister are famous for their cooking, but Heather makes the best potato salad and coleslaw you'll ever taste." She glanced at Zack. "Doesn't she, honey?"

Zack nodded. "It is pretty good."

Kirk took a step back. "Why don't I help you load the truck?"

Zack motioned him around the building. "That would be great."

Kirk followed his friend to the truck around the side of the building. Within minutes, they'd loaded the wood, cement and other items. He noticed Greta and Heather stood beside the passenger's door of the truck. He knew Greta was matchmaking, wanting him to open the door for them. Though tempted to pretend he didn't notice, the manners his mom instilled in him won over, and he obliged. Greta hopped inside the cab and shimmied over toward the middle.

Heather was a bit shorter, so he offered his hand and she hopped into the seat. Her hand shook just a bit in his grasp and she lowered her gaze away from him. She really was a sweet girl. Painfully shy. A little backward. But she was a terrific cook. He knew as much from sampling her food at church fellowships. And she was a hard worker. She helped out with the cleaning and the nursery at the church. If he remembered right, she worked for the daycare downtown.

She'd make someone a good wife. Probably wouldn't leave without a word then refuse to say where she'd been. Most likely wouldn't act all feisty and put out whenever her husband wanted to talk. His life would be so easy if he could fall for a girl like Heather. She would take him as her husband. Cherish him for the rest of her life.

But he didn't love Heather. She wasn't Callie. He waved to Zack as he walked away from the truck and back toward the store. He was done playing games, walking on tiptoe, wondering if Callie was avoiding him.

After purchasing what he needed to fix Old Bertha, he hopped in the truck and headed back to the farm. Callie might not want to talk about what had happened and why she left, but that wouldn't stop him from talking about what his life had been like without her.

Maybe that was what she needed. To hear him say he'd missed her. While they were dating, she'd always gone on and on about being a "words" kind of girl. Something about how she needed to hear him say he loved her, not just have him show it.

He'd never understood why she didn't believe him after he'd said it the first time. He needed to be near her, to see her, to be able wrap her up in his arms. He didn't need to hear her talk about it all the time.

Biting his bottom lip, he inhaled the mixture of cow manure and freshly cut grass, a scent he loved and longed for each spring. He never thought himself a man of words, but he sure did want to know why she'd gone away. It had to be something big, because it hurt him to the core of his being that she'd left him.

Callie slid her hand beneath the strap of the flat brush. She petted Princess's nose then worked the brush down the chestnut quarter horse's neck. Nudging close to the horse's ear, she murmured, "I can't begin to tell you how much I missed you, Princess."

The horse whinnied and tossed her head gently to the side. Callie continued to brush the horse's silky coat. She'd always been the prettiest of horses with her red chestnut coloring, white nose and white stockings that resembled knee-high socks on both of her back legs. Her mane was thick and heavy as ever. Callie patted the horse's flank. "And you look as strong and healthy as the day I left you."

"You can thank Kirk for that."

Callie jumped and placed her hand against her chest at the sound of the male voice behind her. She turned and swatted his arm. "Ben Jacobs, you scared the life right out of me."

Ben chuckled and lifted his hands in surrender. "What? A man can't go into his own barn to do some chores?"

She narrowed her gaze. Ben sounded like his brother with the innocent, and yet oh-so-guilty, question. "Doesn't mean you can sneak up on me." She lifted the flat brush in the air. "What if I'd hauled off and hit you with this?"

Ben winked. "I think I could ward you off."

She pursed her lips and stomped her foot trying to think of a comeback for his insolence. When none came, she sobered when she thought of Ben's words when he'd first come in the barn. "Why'd he keep her alive?"

"She was his link to you." Ben shrugged. "And he loves you."

Callie shook her head. "No. He wrote me off as dead and never came for me."

"That's his pride taking over. You know that as well as I do."

Pain and frustration twisted Callie's gut, and she reached into a nearby bucket and scooped up a handful of oats. She pressed her hand to Princess's mouth, allowing her to enjoy a treat. "How bad was the break?"

"It was pretty bad. Kirk spent several nights in the barn making sure she healed up."

Ben walked closer to her, and Callie looked up at the boy who had been a gangly teenager when she left. Now, he had muscles covering those long arms and legs. He'd grown into his feet and his ball cap. And his eyes rivaled Kirk's for their dark brown intensity. "Why don't you take her for a walk?"

"I can ride her?"

Ben grabbed a saddle off the barn wall and placed it on Princess. "Take it easy on the girl. No racing through the fields, but she's fine to take you out to the pond."

Callie grinned. "How'd you know I'd want to go there?"

"Little brothers are notorious for following their big brothers around." He nudged Callie's arm. "Even when they're fishing and stealing kisses from their girl."

She punched his shoulder then slipped her foot into the stirrup. "You are a total sneak."

He helped her onto the horse's back. "That I am." He patted Princess's rump. "Now go enjoy the sunshine."

The light May breeze blew through her hair, and Callie drank in God's creation. The land shouted of rebirth. New leaves on the trees. Thick green grass from April's watering. Wildflowers blooming in the fields.

The trees parted and she spied the pond. Their pond. How many days had she and Kirk fished in this very spot? Or simply sat and talked, watching frogs hop along the edges? Or enjoyed kisses that must have been witnessed by his little brother?

Warmth raced up her cheeks, and Callie rolled her eyes. She wasn't surprised Ben followed them. He'd always adored Kirk. Followed his every footstep.

She hopped off Princess and tied her to the same tree she'd tied her to more times than she could recall. Dozens upon dozens of times.

She walked to the bank of the pond, slipped off her shoe and touched the water with the tip of her toes. The last time she'd been here, she'd been alone. Just her and God. Not even Princess. She'd poured out her heart to the Lord, still saddened by her mother's death, furious that her father had sent his nephew Bill to request that she go help him because he was sick.

Pushing back her hair with her fingertips, she covered her cheeks with both palms. *I want to forgive him, God. Sometimes I do forgive him. Lay my feelings for him at Your feet. Then I take them back.*

She shook her head, not wanting to think about her dad. God was her refuge in times of trouble. He'd proven it time and again. *And He cares for those who trust in*

Him. The verse from Nahum that she'd memorized, spoken, whispered, muttered for the past five years filled her mind. God had never failed her. Not once.

Her mind replayed the first time she'd seen Kirk since returning to Bloom Hollow. His large frame had filled the room when he'd walked into the house. His stature had always taken her breath. Made her feel safe and secure. For a moment, she'd seen something in his gaze, maybe the love they'd once shared. Then his gaze had hardened, and he'd proclaimed that she was dead in his eyes.

She bit her bottom lip as his words suddenly struck her as funny. Ben was right. Kirk had as much pride as he did body. A man didn't need that much. It would never do him much good. Only cause a lot of unnecessary pain.

He'd loved her once upon a time. She knew he had. She walked toward Princess and petted her nose. And maybe keeping her horse alive showed that he still loved her. But she wasn't ready for all that. She was broken. Worn out. Weary to her core. And the only One who could help her was the Lord.

Walking back to the pond, she slipped out of both shoes and sat down on the bank. She placed her hands against the firm earth and stuck her feet in the edge of the cool water. Lifting her face to the heavens, she closed her eyes. "God, fill me with Your presence. Clean me up, Lord. Make my faith strong again. I need Your joy."

She wasn't much of a singer, but a contemporary song about God's amazing love floated through her mind, and Callie lifted her voice in praise. She still felt as weak as Princess must have been with a broken leg, but her heart was starting to fill up again. Not enough to go back to her nursing job or to run back into Kirk's arms, but enough to get her through another day. Maybe even a week. However long, she knew God still cared for her.

Chapter 6

Kirk loved kids. Never minded having a slew of them running around the farm. He enjoyed watching boys and girls slide down the slides, climb the hay bale mountain, swing on oversize swings and spin on the merry-go-round. His heart warmed each time he saw a girl's eyes light up when a goat ate from her hand or a boy cheer as he rode a pony.

Middle school kids were a different story altogether. Every year the local middle school brought their seventh graders for an end-of-the-year field trip. Every year Kirk dreaded it.

Inevitably, a group of girls would act snide and cruel to another group of girls, or in worst cases, a single girl. Boys would try to show each other up on the playground, and someone would wind up injured or destroying property. They had to watch for stolen kisses and fistfights behind the hay bales. And though much older than the other students who visit the farm, seventh graders left the biggest mess and made the most noise. Part of him wished Mom would stop saying they could come. Course he knew if she did, there'd be a ton of community members none too happy with them.

He harrumphed, noting the few chaperones for the two hundred kids. Only teachers. Parents must not be overly excited to spend the day with their adolescents, either.

"Hey, Mr. Jacobs."

He glanced at the scrawny, dark-haired girl with an aluminum smile. She giggled as she gripped her blonde-haired friend's arm. "My friend thinks you're cute."

He bit back a growl as the blonde girl's face turned bright red before she squealed and raced away from her friend.

Kirk rolled his eyes when the dark-haired girl chased after the blonde one. He spied Ben beside the petting area. His brother had a couple of girls surrounding him. Kirk knew Ben received even more young adolescent attention than he did. It was a blessed day when his younger brother became the heartthrob of the family, and Kirk would miss Ben next year if he didn't make it home for the middle school field trip.

He made his way to the hay bale mountain and walked around it. A short kid with dark brown hair pointed to a tall, lanky boy wearing a middle school baseball team T-shirt. Several other boys stood around them, all sporting the same shirt. "Ain't nobody gonna beat Tyler. He's the fastest kid in seventh grade."

The sandy-haired kid grinned, exposing a big gap in his two front teeth. He lifted his chin, and Kirk noticed a couple girls standing a few feet away, ogling the obvious jock of the grade. Kirk bit back a grin at the boy. Cocky as a rooster in a hen house, but built like a foal that still hadn't grown into his legs.

Another boy, this one a bit on the chunky side, patted another kid's shoulders. That kid looked a little familiar, and Kirk furrowed his brows trying to place him. "Bet he can't beat Justin. He works on his pa's farm every day."

Kirk nodded. Yep. He knew the kid. He was Tim Reynolds's boy. Owned the farm a few miles over. Kirk hadn't realized his boy had gotten so big. The last time he'd paid attention to the kid, he'd been no taller than Kirk's hip. Course, he was still a bit on the small side, but Kirk had no doubt the boy was scrappy. He knew Tim made his kids work hard on the farm.

Only one other boy stood with Justin and his friend. It was an obvious match of the jocks versus the country boys. Kirk bit the inside of his mouth as he remembered his middle school days. He'd never played sports, too busy working the farm, and he'd loved working the farm. But, oh, how the jocks used to burn him up. If he'd wanted to take them on, he could have showed them what real work was.

Kirk grinned. If he was a betting man, his money would be on Justin.

"Let 'em race, then," said the short kid as he patted Tyler's shoulder.

Justin glanced at the group of girls watching the boys' bantering. Kirk wondered if Justin had a crush on one of the girls. He remembered his crush in seventh grade. Took all the way to sophomore year to get over that girl. Then he'd seen the freshman, Callie, for the first time.

A flash of pain whipped through his gut. Still hadn't gotten over that freshman girl.

"I'm ready if he is." Justin leaned forward with his elbows bent and his left foot forward.

Tyler blew out a breath. "This will be a breeze." He leaned forward, as well.

Kirk bit his tongue to keep from cheering for Justin. He crossed his arms in front of his chest. His mom probably wouldn't let the boys race, but as long as no one got angry or acted foolish, he didn't think there was any harm in a bit of competition.

"All right, then," the chubby boy announced. He clapped his hands together. "On your mark—"

Shorty held up his hand. "I'll say go. Not you."

The chubby kid lifted his hands. "No problem. Either way Justin's gonna show you up."

Kirk grinned. He wished he'd had that much confidence in middle school. Man, that was an awkward time in his life.

"On your mark. Get set. Go!"

The boys took off. Tyler's long legs should have given him an advantage lifting himself from one hay bale to the next, but Justin had done this before. He'd spent his life climbing over and around hay bales. He scaled the mountain easily. He was on his way back down while Tyler still hadn't reached the top.

Justin jumped off the bottom hay bale and Chubby and their other friend patted his back. Chubby turned toward the boys. "Told ya he could beat him."

Kirk snarled as the baseball boys didn't acknowledge the country guys and walked toward the other side of the hay bale mountain, where Tyler had jumped down. The ball crew couldn't even lose like men.

Kirk cocked his head. Probably because they weren't men. They were boys. Full of energy and competitiveness and an inability to know how to handle all of it. He walked up to the threesome and patted Justin's shoulder. "Good job scaling that mountain. I reckon your dad would be proud to see how fast you made it up there and back."

Justin's gaze lingered the slightest moment on the couple girls who followed the group of baseball players to the slides. He looked up at Kirk. "You know my dad?"

"Sure. You're Tim's boy, aren't you?"

He nodded.

"Tell him I said hello." Kirk lifted his hand and Justin gave him a high-five. "Good win."

The boy grinned, and Kirk watched as he and his friends walked toward the petting area. Pamela seemed to have her hands full with a group of girls trying to feed too much to Old Tom. The dumb goat wouldn't stop eating even if his stomach was about to explode.

"Uncle Kirk! Come quick!"

Kirk jumped at the urgency in his youngest niece's voice. "What is it?"

"It's Grandma. She fell." Tears raced down Emmy's cheeks. "Something is wrong."

"Where?"

"She's on the front porch. She fell and..."

Kirk didn't wait for his niece's explanation. He ran to the house.

Callie flattened the quilt on the bed in one of the guest rooms of the main home that they also used as a bed-and-breakfast. They'd named this room the Sunshine Room, and it was by far her favorite. The pinwheel quilt reminded her of the sun with its various shades of yellow and splashes of orange-and-salmon colors. Long yellow curtains pulled back with oversize white bows gave the room an overly feminine feeling. The clean white walls appealed to Callie's need for refreshment in her life. A taupe wingback chair sat in the corner beside an end table and lamp contraption. The lamp shade matched the curtains, even had a white bow tied around the bottom of the yellow fabric. A velvety afghan was draped over the back of the chair and a devotional book was placed in the seat.

"Mom, what happened?"

Kirk's voice boomed up the stairs. He sounded as if he was on the front porch. Peeking out the window, she spied Tammie sitting on the ground holding her leg. Callie raced down the stairs and out the front door.

"I fell off the porch. I don't even know how I did it."

Tammie's voice shook, and Callie noted tears pooling in her eyes. Her khaki capris were ripped at the hem. A stream of blood flowed from her knee down her calf. Already her ankle appeared swollen, and Callie feared this injury would require more than tweezers and a butterfly bandage.

"I got help, Grandma." Emmy ran from the playground area and grabbed hold of Kirk's hand.

Callie glanced at Kirk. His face had turned pasty-white, and he seemed frozen in place. A lot of good these Jacobs men were.

Callie shook her head. "Emmy, go get me a wash rag and a big bowl of warm water." She nudged Kirk's arm. "You could help her, if you'd like." She snapped her fingers. "And I'll need a bag of ice, too."

Kirk guided Emmy into the house, and Callie knelt

beside Tammie. She gently pushed the capris farther away from Tammie's knee. "So, what hurts?"

"My ankle." Tammie bit her bottom lip, and Callie knew her friend fought to keep her composure.

"I thought so."

"I think it's broken."

"I do, too."

"It snapped."

Callie nodded. "Then it's probably broken."

Tammie's lips curved up ever so slightly, though she continued to bite the bottom one. "I'm glad you're here."

"Me, too. I think Kirk would have just stood there looking at you."

Tammie nodded. "Most likely. Mike's the only one who holds it together when one of us gets hurt."

"Where is he? I thought he was with Kirk, Pamela and Ben and the middle school kids."

"Went to town. Sink isn't working in one of the guest bathrooms." A large tear escaped, and she swiped it away. "We have two couples coming to the B and B tomorrow night."

"Don't you worry a moment about that. Everything will be ready. We'll make sure of it." Callie looked around her shoulder at the front of the house. Where were Kirk and Emmy? All she'd asked for was a bowl of water, a washcloth and some ice.

The door flung open, and Emmy bounded out with a washcloth in one hand and a bag of ice in the other. The door sprang back and hit Kirk's hands, splashing water all over his shirt and pants. Emmy lifted her shoulders. "Sorry, Uncle Kirk."

He didn't respond as he pushed open the door then brought the bowl to Callie. She gently placed the bag of ice on Tammie's ankle then took the washcloth, dipped it in water and wrung it out. She blotted Tammie's scuffed knee, ensuring to get all the dirt and any pebbles out of the spot, then wiped off her leg. "Emmy, do you know where the bandages are?"

Emmy nodded.

"Will you go get me a big one for Grandma's knee?"

She nodded again then raced back into the house.

Callie looked at Kirk. "She's going to have to go to the hospital."

"Why?"

"I think my ankle's broken." Tammie winced and sucked in her breath.

Callie touched her arm. "Don't talk. Just focus on breathing. You're doing a great job holding it together in front of Emmy." She stopped herself from adding, "And Kirk." The guy still looked like he could star in a ghost movie.

Kirk stood. "Fine. I'll get the truck."

Callie stood beside him. "I'm taking her."

"No, you're not."

"Yes, I am."

"Callie, I don't know what makes you think you can just waltz back into our lives and—"

She touched his arm. "Look at you, Kirk. You're shaking like a leaf. You'll wreck and hurt both of you."

"I will not."

"You will."

"I'm taking her, and that's final."

"Kirk, you're being ridiculous. I'm a nurse."

"There are nurses at the hospital."

"I know that, but—"

"She's my mother."

"She's like a mother to me."

"A good way you have of showing it. Leaving without a word for five years."

Tammie clapped her hands. "That's enough. I'll not listen to another word." She winced again, and a shiver of guilt slipped through Callie for fussing with Kirk in front of her. "Callie will take me to the hospital. Kirk, you will help your sister finish out the middle school field trip."

Callie lifted her chin and squared her shoulders, preparing to argue with Kirk if he continued. He narrowed his gaze and stared at her for a moment before blowing out a breath. "Fine. I'll bring the truck up here and Callie can take you."

"Kirk, we have guests coming tomorrow. I don't want you leaving tire track marks in the yard. Can't you just carry me to the truck?"

"What if I hurt you?"

Callie stifled a chuckle at the sudden panic that wrapped his features. Taunting him, she said, "Big guy like you can't carry his own mama."

Kirk sneered, and Callie almost laughed out loud. She loved goading him. It didn't take much. One time she'd watched him jump three feet in the air when a garden snake slithered over his boot. She'd teased him for weeks until… She sobered. She didn't want to think about those times with Kirk. That was a long time ago. A lot had changed since then.

"I'll be fine," said Tammie. "Just put your hand under my knees and around my back."

Before he lifted her, Emmy ran out the front door holding a large bandage. Callie took the bandage and put it on Tammie's knee. Even with the ice covering it,

Callie noticed the ankle had swollen more. The doctor wouldn't be able to do anything until the swelling went down, but they could still determine the severity of the break and also give her some pain medication.

"Run on back and tell your mom everything is fine," said Kirk. "I'll be right over there in a minute."

While Emmy raced back to the playground area, Kirk carried Tammie to the truck, and Callie hopped into the driver's seat. After easing her down, he kissed his mom's forehead. Longing niggled at Callie's heart as she wished to be cared for so much.

"Take care of her," he said.

Callie lifted one eyebrow. "You mean your mom or the truck, 'cause if I remember right you had mighty strong feelings about your vehicles."

Kirk growled, and Tammie released a laugh and a wince at the same time.

Callie sobered. "You know I'll take care of Tammie."

"I'll tell Pamela and Ben what's going on, and I'll text Dad." He looked at Callie. The concern for his mom she saw on his face tugged at her heartstrings again, and she fought the urge to tell him to come around the truck and give her a kiss, as well. "Call me when you know something," he said.

"Oh, for Pete's sake, I'm not dead." Tammie swatted his arm. "Go help your brother and sister."

Callie started the truck and waved at Kirk. She bit her bottom lip as she remembered how he'd once worried over her like he did his mom.

Chapter 7

He saw it in her eyes. For only a moment. But it was there. The love she'd once felt for him. Maybe it wasn't love just yet, but she still felt something. He knew it.

He pulled out his cell phone and texted his dad about Callie taking Mom to the hospital then walked back toward the play area and petting zoo. Jacobs Family Farm had seen more activity in the past few weeks than he could remember in a while. Callie's return. Little Timmy's injury. Now his mom's ankle. Normally, life ran smooth. Consistent. Same routine day in and day out. He wasn't one for change, but each day he found himself happier that Callie had returned.

She'd been attending church with them. Not once had she chosen the seat beside him, but having her there, in the pew with the family, had filled him with a peace he hadn't felt in years. When she'd left, she'd taken a piece of him with her.

His phone vibrated in his pocket. He pulled it out and read the caller ID. "Hi, Dad. She's okay. She stepped off—"

"What happened? Did she fall? What was she doing?"

Kirk pulled the phone away from his ear, while his dad ranted. Dad had always been overly protective of Mom. When his dad took a breath, he tried again. "She stepped off the porch weird. Ankle is probably broken."

He pulled the phone away again as Dad continued his rampage of questions. He sounded angry, but Kirk knew it was concern coming over the line. He reacted the same way when it came to Callie. All gruff and grumbles, but deep down it was pain and fear that ate at his insides.

"Go on over to the hospital, Dad. We'll all meet you there as soon as the students leave."

It took a few minutes, but once he was able to get off the phone, Kirk joined his sister and brother. The students loaded into the buses while Kirk, Pamela and Ben cleaned up.

"What did she do?" asked Ben.

"Looks like she broke her ankle."

"How?" Pamela knotted an overflowing bag of trash and pulled it out of the container.

Kirk picked up two plastic cups off the ground and placed them in the second trash can. "Would you believe stepping off the porch?"

Ben laughed. "I would believe it."

Pamela placed her hands on her hips. "Ben Jacobs, this is not funny. Summer is starting, and you know how much work Mom and I have to do at the bed-and-breakfast and the café."

"It'll be fine. Callie's here." Ben grabbed a paper towel from the picnic table and used it to pull a wad of bubble gum off the seat. "Maybe this will make Mom slow down a bit. She works too hard."

Kirk exchanged glances with Pamela. They both knew Ben was right. Mom battled high blood pressure, and she'd been more stressed the past few months. The only reason Kirk could figure was because Ben had decided to attend the University of Tennessee this fall, which meant he was the first of her kids to move a couple hours away. Since Callie's return, Mom had been concerned about her, too. Though he would have never asked for his mom to break her ankle, maybe it would settle her down.

Pamela shrugged. "Might even slow Dad down a bit."

Emmy tugged on Kirk's shirt. "Are we gonna go see Grandma?"

He picked her up and tapped her nose with his fingertip. "Yes, we are. As soon as we get everything cleaned up and Emma gets off the bus."

"Is Grandma okay?"

"Of course she is." He put her back on the ground. "Help clean up so we can go see her faster."

Kirk and Ben tended the animals while Pamela and Emmy finished cleaning up the play area. Knowing guests were scheduled to stay at the B and B the following day, he hoped they had everything they needed at the main house. *I'm sure Mom will tell us if we need to get anything. She's probably driving Callie crazy.*

He imagined Callie scribbling a list of needed items on a hospital notepad. If his dad had arrived, he'd be giving her an earful, as well. But Callie would take it in stride. Always willing to help and take care of people; it was one of the things he'd loved about her.

Pamela walked up beside him. “Do you recognize this number?”

He looked down at her cell phone and then shook his head.

“Me neither. I’ve gotten a call from it three times this week.”

“Call it back and see who it is.”

“I have. No one answers and no voice mail.”

“Block it.”

“I would—”

“But you think it might be Jack.” Kirk grabbed his sister’s hand. “You’re better off without him.”

“I know that.” Pamela frowned. “But he’s still the girls’ dad.”

“He’s never been a dad to those girls. He’s never even seen Emmy. I’m glad he’s gone.”

Pamela glanced down at the ground. “I know.”

Kirk bit back a growl. His sister still pined after a man who drank more than he worked and who ran out on her and the girls. And yet Kirk had been good to Callie all the years they’d dated. Sure, he’d experienced a couple months of panic, but he couldn’t get her to consider him again.

Emma’s bus pulled in front of the house. He grabbed Pamela’s hand. “Come on. Let’s go to the hospital and see about Mom.”

“I still can’t believe Mom broke her ankle just stepping off the porch.” Ben took a bite of his hot fudge sundae.

Callie rocked on the front porch swing. She breathed in the cool spring evening air and smiled at the conversation between Kirk, Pamela and Ben. With Kirk’s parents and the girls tucked soundly in bed, it had been a long time since Callie enjoyed the crescent moon and a sky full of stars. Despite the busyness of the day, she relished the simplicity of Bloom Hollow.

"I can believe it," Pamela said. "She's constantly getting bruises from running into one thing or another."

"That doesn't mean broken bones," said Ben.

"Might as well," said Pamela. "She did it this time, didn't she?"

"What are you thinking about over there?"

The sound of Kirk's voice drew her from her reverie, and she realized all three of them were looking at her. Releasing a deep sigh, she said, "Just how much I missed this place."

Kirk's gaze drew her, and she knew he wanted to know more. She looked at Ben and Pamela. "And how much I missed you all and listening to you talk with each other."

"We missed you, too," whispered Pamela.

"Yeah, and I didn't have a date to the senior prom. Remember you promised to go with me?"

Ben stuck out his bottom lip, and Callie chuckled. "I stood you up, didn't I? I'm sorry."

She sneaked a peek at Kirk. He still studied her. "How was it as a hospice nurse?"

"Hard and good." She stared past the porch at the mountain range. "My last client, Frank, was a sixty-five-year-old widower with four kids, five grandkids and suffering with pancreatic cancer. He loved to tease that he and I would have had a fling if he were forty years younger, and if I wasn't younger than two of his grandchildren." She smiled, remembering his toothless grin and bushy eyebrows. "When he died, I knew I had to take a break for a while."

Pamela wrapped the afghan higher around her shoulders. "I bet you were a terrific nurse. You have such a caring nature."

She glanced at Kirk again. He didn't say anything, simply watched her. Tonight, she didn't mind. Maybe it was exhaustion or maybe she was beginning to heal. Whatever it was, she simply didn't mind. "I enjoyed it. I'll do it again one day. Just not yet."

Silence wrapped itself around them, and Callie sucked in more of the clean Tennessee air. She should go to bed. Tammie had given them all a list of chores to accomplish before the guests arrived tomorrow afternoon. They needed their rest, and yet the evening felt so nice.

"It's nights like these I miss Jack."

"Oh, Pamela."

"I can't help it, Ben." Pamela sat up straighter in the wicker chair. "I know you and Kirk and Mom and Dad don't approve, but it wasn't always bad with him. We had good moments. When he wasn't drinking, we had lots of them." She folded her hands in her lap. "We loved to sit outside together on nice spring evenings."

"What happened?" Callie looked at each of the brothers when she asked the question, unsure if they would be mad at her question. Both remained quiet, though, obviously perturbed.

"Alcohol. That's what happened. Jack couldn't stop drinking, and when he drank he was mean." She raised her hand. "He never hit me or Emma, but he did scare me real good the last time. I told him to leave. He did, and I haven't heard from him since."

Ben growled. "That's 'cause he's a no-good—"

"I thought I'd never see my dad again," Callie said.

Ben hushed at her words. Callie looked at Kirk. He watched her, his gaze begging her to continue. And why shouldn't she tell them. She'd said the words aloud to God so many times, and He had healed her. Maybe saying them to someone else would help her to stop taking the pain back. "That was why Bill came. To tell me Dad was dying. Pancreatic cancer. Just like Frank."

"And you went to him."

The comment came from Kirk, and she looked at him. "Yes, and I should have come to the farm and told you all." She clasped her hands. "At the time, I felt angry and numb. It's hard to explain. I went to help him out of duty. I tried to forgive him. Begged God to help me forgive him for leaving Mom and me."

"But you couldn't," said Pamela.

"I think I did." Callie shrugged. "There's always something else, though. Life never stays easy. Guess that's why we have to stay dependent on God."

"Very true," said Pamela.

Callie stood. "I'm starting to get tired. I think I'll head to the cabin."

"I'll walk with you."

Before Callie could protest, Kirk was beside her, holding her elbow in his hand. He didn't talk as they made the short trek to the cabin. Callie's heart pounded in her chest at the overwhelming feeling of vulnerability. She felt weak tonight, in need of physical comfort. A hug. A kiss. She focused on the crunching of the grass beneath their feet and the crickets that chirped all around them.

They stopped in front of the door, and Callie reached

in her front jeans pocket for the key. She avoided Kirk's gaze as she unlocked the door. "Thanks for walking me back."

Kirk grabbed her hand. "Wait. There's more. What else happened?"

Callie couldn't look up at his face. She stared at his chest or beyond him. "I think watching your mom and your dad die battling cancer is enough, don't you?"

"Absolutely." He cupped her chin, and she had to gaze up into his truth-seeking eyes. "But there is more."

"It's selfish. And embarrassing."

"I'm sure it's not."

Callie exhaled a deep breath. Her defenses were down. She was tired of putting on a facade of strength. She wanted understanding. Comfort.

Gazing down at her feet, she whispered, "My dad left everything in his will to my uncle and cousin Bill. Nothing to me."

She shook her head. "It's ridiculous that it bothers me so much. I didn't need his money or his house or his car. I made a good salary as a nurse. But I thought we'd bonded again. I was with him when he died, but when the lawyer read the will…" She swatted the air. "See what I mean. Totally selfish of me."

"That's not selfish, Cals."

She peered up at him. Ben had called her the old nickname often since she returned, but Kirk hadn't. Hearing it from his lips sent a shiver down her spine. Strong fingers raked through her hair until he held the back of her head in his palms. "I love…"

He couldn't say it. She wasn't ready to hear the words slip from lips she'd dreamed about practically every night as a teenager. And as a young woman. Even when she tried to forget him, his lips haunted her.

She had to stop him. Standing on tiptoe, she grabbed his head in her hands and pulled him down to her. Capturing his lips with hers, she gasped at the emotion that welled inside her at kissing him again.

She tried to back away from him, but Kirk grabbed her around the waist and pulled her close. She relished his embrace. Drank in the musky scent of his cologne, the soft urgency of his lips against hers. It felt so good to be in his arms again.

But she wasn't ready. She didn't want to be vulnerable. If she didn't love, she didn't lose. Pulling away from his embrace, she nodded and opened the door. "Good night, Kirk."

Kirk opened his mouth, but Callie slipped into the house and shut the door. After turning the lock, she leaned against it. *Stopping him from saying I love you by laying a big one on him might not have been the wisest of choices. He'll definitely have the wrong impression now.*

She touched her lips. She was torturing herself, as well. *It took years to push his kiss to the back of my mind. Now, I'll never forget.*

Chapter 8

"God, I love her." Kirk couldn't keep the smile from his lips as he hopped into the tractor. Truth be told, he didn't even want to. It had been years since he'd felt Callie's sweet mouth pressed against his. He'd missed the pleasure.

The sun shone bright over God's creation, and Kirk's chest swelled at the blossoming orchard, apple and peach trees that lined his family's land for acres. Past the barn, he knew the strawberry plants bore their fruit while the blackberry bushes grew in preparation of their later harvest time.

Two older couples were already set up in the B and B. Knowing Callie was there caring for his mother and ensuring their guests enjoyed a nice lunch made him dizzy with contentment.

He had all a man wanted in life. A job. A home. And a good woman.

And of course, You, Lord. Having a relationship with You makes my life complete.

He started up the tractor. Normally, he used earphones and listened to a western novel on CD. Today, he couldn't stifle the worship bubbling up in his heart and mind. Despite warring with the tractor for volume, in a deep baritone voice he bellowed, "'When peace like a river attendeth my way, when sorrows like sea billows roll.'"

He shifted gears on the tractor and turned to see the Smoky Mountains rising and falling as the backdrop to his home. Peace wrapped around him. "'Whatever my lot, Thou has taught me to say, it is well. It is well with my soul.'"

He finished the chores then shut the barn door. Anxious to get back to the main house, he wanted to see Callie, to help her with their guests, to work with her. He'd always believed they worked well together. She'd had such a bubbly, caring nature. True, he hadn't seen the bubbly side of her since she'd returned. And he'd noticed she seemed to shut off her caring side when she helped Timmy and even his mom with their injuries.

But that would change once she'd been home a little while. Dealing with her mom's and then her dad's deaths. Then working with death day in and day out. Well, it was enough to make anyone a bit solemn. The clean, fresh country air would change that. After being with him, as she allowed him to love her again, she'd go back to her old self.

"Kirk, can you help me a minute?"

He looked at his sister who stood at the front door of the café and gift shop. She had a paintbrush in one hand

and motioned for him with the other. His chest fell. He knew Pamela had been trying to finish whitewashing the café's walls before the crowds started when school let out next week.

Walking toward her, he took off his ball cap and wiped his forehead with the back of his hand. "Sure, sis. What do you need?"

"We have some new inventory to put in the shop. Sue's quilt and crochet pieces. And Terri brought over some new jewelry she made. They need to be set up." She lifted the paint can. "You want to paint or inventory?"

"Did you even need to ask?"

Pamela giggled. "Nope." She handed him the brush and can. "Just thought I'd give you the option."

"I don't know what to do with all that girly stuff."

"But you're a fantastic painter." She punched his arm. "So hop to it."

He dipped the brush in the paint, pressed the excess off on the side of the can then formed even strokes along the edge of the baseboard. "Where are the girls?"

"Helping Callie and Dad make lunch. I hope they're not driving her crazy."

He put down the brush and wiped his hands. "I'll go check. I'll send Dad out here to help. He paints better than me, anyway."

"First off," Pamela said, "you know Dad's not going to leave Mom alone after just breaking her ankle yesterday. And second, you need to give Callie some time. You're pressuring her too much."

"She kissed me."

He bit the inside of his lip as soon as the words left his mouth. It wasn't Pamela's business. He didn't want her snooping around in his affairs, and he didn't need to endure all her advice.

"She kissed you?"

He tried to ignore her question. Picked up the brush and started on the wall again.

Pamela didn't back off. "Wonder why? Were you pestering her to death? Trying to get her to open up about everything in her life?"

Frustration welled within him, but his mind replayed the night before. Was she just trying to get him to stop talking? He shook his head. No. That wasn't what happened. "Now listen, Pamela—"

Pamela's phone rang, and she plucked it from her pocket. Grimacing, she showed him the screen. "It's that number again. It's called three times today."

Kirk frowned and grabbed the phone from her hand. He pushed the talk button. "Hello. Who is this?"

"Who is this?" a man answered.

Anger washed over him as he recognized the voice. "I suggest you stop calling this number."

Before the guy could respond, Kirk ended the call. "You need to block that number from your phone."

"It's Jack, isn't it?"

Aggravation with his sister warred with the anger streaming through his veins. "If you knew it was him, why didn't you block the number before?"

Pamela shrugged. "I suppose because of the girls."

"He sounded drunk, sis."

"Just then?"

Kirk nodded.

"Guess I'm not surprised."

Kirk's feelings deflated at the wounded expression

on her face. He wrapped his arms around her. "You gotta let him go."

"I have, but that doesn't mean it doesn't hurt."

"Why don't we both go to the house and check on how Callie and Dad are doing with lunch? I'll come help you afterward."

Pamela nodded, and he guided her out the door. His own words replayed in his mind. He'd told Pamela to let Jack go. His sister and parents kept telling him to give Callie time to heal, to let her go until she was ready.

But that didn't apply now. Callie had come back. She'd opened up to him and his siblings last night. She'd kissed him with the same fervency he remembered from years ago. Somehow, last night tasted sweeter, and he couldn't wait for a replay tonight.

He followed Pamela into the house. Spying Callie at the sink washing strawberries, he made his way to her. He tweaked the tip of her ponytail. "Hey."

She pulled her hair from his grasp. "Hi."

He frowned. Her reception seemed a bit gruffer than he'd anticipated. Probably because she was busy trying to get lunch on the table. "Can I help?"

"Wash your hands and set the table."

Dread niggled at his chest. She seemed more than gruff. She was distancing herself again. But why? What did the woman want? For him to proclaim his dying love for her? He'd do it if that was what she needed. The next time they were alone, he'd tell her exactly how he felt.

She's come back, Lord. And I'm not letting her go again. I was a fool the first time. I won't make the same mistakes.

A vision of his dad teaching him, as a boy, the tricks

to breaking a horse played through his mind. "Patience," his dad had said. "Gotta be patient."

Patience had never been one of Kirk's stronger qualities.

Callie dabbed her eyes with a wet washcloth. She gripped the vanity sink in the bathroom and stared at her reflection. She'd lain awake most of the night over that kiss. How could she have been so foolish, so impulsive?

She had no desire to get back together with Kirk. Well, that wasn't exactly true. She had loads of desire, but a relationship was not what she wanted. Or needed. The people she loved died. All of them.

Shrugging, she washed her hands in the sink. Death was a part of life. Everyone died. But the people she loved died too early, and she simply couldn't handle any more heartbreak.

She shouldn't have kissed him. It was a mistake. Now, she didn't know if she should apologize or simply pretend it never happened. If she apologized, he might look down at her with those enticing eyes, which seemed to have a knack for drawing her into them, and then she'd end up throwing herself in his arms again. She shook her head. No, she couldn't risk that. Ignoring him would infuriate him, but she wasn't tempted to kiss him when he was angry. Not nearly as much, anyway.

After drying her hands, she joined the family in the kitchen. The visitors had been fed and cleaned up after. They'd already left to enjoy some hiking. Mike and Tammie sat at the kitchen table, as did Ben and the girls. Tammie's leg was propped on a chair. Her brows furrowed and her face flushed. She'd been up the whole morning. She needed to eat and then rest a bit. Callie looked at the kitchen clock. "Tammie, I'll get you some pain pills so that after you eat you can lie down for a while."

"I think I'll do that." Her hand shook when she picked up a glass of iced tea and took a drink.

Mike grimaced. "I wish I could make it better."

"I know." Tammie patted the top of his hand. "It will get better once they can set it and put on the cast."

"Grandma, I'll go fluff your pillows," said Emma, and she raced into the other room.

Emmy hopped up. "I'll go put my panda bear on your bed. He likes to take naps."

Callie's heart swelled at the tenderness of the family. Pamela placed plates of hot ham and cheese, potato salad and cole slaw in front of her parents. Kirk filled glasses with sweet tea then sat beside Ben. Two seats left. One beside him. One beside Ben.

Before Pamela could choose, Callie grabbed a plate and sat beside Ben. She glanced at Kirk, noting the frown wrapping his features. Ugh, she wanted to scream. He had every right to be confused and frustrated with her. Why couldn't she have just told him to mind his own business and slammed the door in his face last night?

"Ben, is everything ready for school in the fall? All the paperwork turned in?" asked Mike.

Callie breathed a sigh of relief. If they talked about normal stuff, maybe she could eat quickly then head upstairs to make the guest beds and tidy up the bathrooms.

Ben swallowed the bite of hot ham and cheese. He wiped his mouth with a napkin. "I think so, Dad. Transfer scholarship papers are completed. Classes are ready. In just a few months, I'll be working toward my engineering degree."

Kirk ruffled Ben's hair. "The nerd of the family's headin' off to school."

Pamela released an exaggerated sigh, and Callie studied the woman she once believed would be her sister-in-law. There were only a few months between their ages, and though she'd always liked Pamela, they'd never spent a lot of time together. The main reason had been because Pamela had spent all of her time with Jack.

After swallowing a bite of potato salad, Callie asked, "Did you want to go to school, Pamela?"

She nodded, but didn't offer a comment, simply took another bite of her sandwich.

"She wanted to be a math teacher." Tammie placed her hand on Pamela's arm. "Isn't that right? Then it was..." She lifted her finger to her mouth. "What was it?"

"An accountant." Pamela continued to focus on her plate. "I wanted to be an accountant."

Callie swallowed a drink of her tea. "Then go back. Take a few classes at the community college. I'll help you get started."

Pamela looked up at Callie, a slight smile lifting her lips. "It's not so easy with the girls, and—"

"They'll both be in school this fall. I bet you could take a class or two. I'm here to help around the house, and—"

Mike patted Pamela's back. "I think it's a wonderful idea. You're great with numbers. You take care of our books just fine."

"You should do it, sis," said Ben.

Pamela blushed, and Callie noticed she seemed to try to shrink back into a shell. Callie wouldn't let her.

"Later on, you and I are going to print out an application and fill it out. Okay?"

Pamela shrugged. "I don't know. We'll see."

Tammie released a loud sigh. "I'm sorry to be such a downer at our lunch party, but I think my medicine is kicking in." She turned toward Mike. "Will you help me up? I need to get to the bed, or I'll be facedown in this plate in a minute."

Mike chuckled as he helped his wife into the bedroom. Ben excused himself to finish working in the barn. Callie swallowed a knot in her throat and begged God that Pamela and the girls wouldn't leave the table. She shoved another bite of ham and cheese in her mouth. If she hadn't talked so much during lunch, she'd be finished and could excuse herself, as well.

"Mama, can I go play? I'm done," said Emmy.

Pamela pointed to the plate. "Two more bites." She pointed at Emma's also. "Both of you."

The girls shoved bites in their mouths, and Callie did the same with an oversize forkful of potato salad.

"Done!" the girls chimed in unison.

Pamela stood, picked up their plates and placed them in the sink. "Okay. Play quietly in your room so Grandma can rest."

With a quiet squeal of consent, the girls raced out of the kitchen. *Please God, let Pamela sit back down. I can't be alone with Kirk.*

She peeked at him. He wasn't going to budge. He probably even prayed against her—that Pamela would leave. She shoved another bite of salad in her mouth.

As Callie expected, Pamela wiped her hands on a dish towel. "I'm heading back to the gift shop. See ya in a bit."

Before Callie could utter a peep, Pamela left. Kirk stood and placed his plate in the sink. Callie sucked in a breath. Maybe he'd leave. Maybe she wouldn't have to worry about explaining or apologizing.

Both his hands cupped her shoulders from behind. "I thought they'd never leave."

Callie swallowed. She'd have to talk to him. Just say something to get him to go away. Like a coward, she stared at her plate. If she looked up at him, she'd melt, and she had to stay strong. "I'm sorry for kissing you last night."

"What?"

Frustration flowed from the single word. She knew him. It would shift to anger in a moment's time. Good. She could avoid him better when he was angry.

"I shouldn't have done it."

"But?"

"No buts." She stood. She couldn't risk looking back at him. Leaving her plate on the table, she walked toward the living room. "I've got work to do."

Chapter 9

Two weeks had passed since Callie kissed him then brushed it off as if it should have never happened. He'd run the gamut of emotions—frustration to anger to aggravation to confusion to peace. Just as she wanted, he'd avoided her. Given her space and then he stuck God in her spot in his mind.

He couldn't remember a time in his life when he'd prayed so much. Ended up, he didn't only pray about Callie. He got to going on about his mom's ankle healing, his brother's school, his dad, his sister and his nieces. He'd always prayed over the land, but he'd taken to actually going out in the orchard, standing right there in the middle of it and lifting his face to the heavens in prayer.

Having been raised on the Bible, he knew it said that he could have a peace that surpassed all understanding. But he'd never understood that before. The peace he now felt didn't make any sense. It was as if anything in the world could happen and he knew God would see him through it.

And he'd never felt more love for Callie. Real love. The kind that gave her space and didn't demand to fill it. The kind that wanted the very best for her. Wanted her to be ready to come to him. The kind of love God had for the world.

Having finished the farm work, Kirk headed to his house to clean up before dinner. The B and B had a cancellation, so it would just be the family. No waiting on guests. No sitting all crowded together at the kitchen table.

He walked inside as Ben squirted cologne on his shirt. Kirk whistled at his clean-shaven brother decked out in a royal blue polo shirt and khaki shorts. "Where you going? Hot date?"

"As a matter of fact, yep."

Kirk lifted his brows. "Really?"

Ben scoffed. "Well, don't act so surprised. I *can* get a date, you know."

"Oh, I know. You just said you weren't messing with women. At least until after you got to school."

"And I'm not." Ben blew out a breath. "Stan begged me to go out with his girlfriend's sister who's visiting from Idaho or Iowa or one of the *I* states." He adjusted the collar of his shirt. "But I'm going to kick his rear if the girl has four eyes or a tail. I didn't want to do this to begin with."

"Or she could be gorgeous, latch on and want to marry you."

Ben growled. "That would be worse." He furrowed his brows. "Wait. Not the gorgeous part. The latch on and marry part."

Kirk laughed as he made his way to the bathroom. "Have fun."

"You know Pamela and the girls are going to a birthday party tonight."

Kirk stopped. That meant only his parents, Callie and he would have supper together.

"And Dad took Mom out for dinner. First time she felt like she could maneuver on the crutches enough to go out."

Kirk scrunched his face as he scratched the side of his head.

"That leaves just you and Callie."

"Yeah. I did the math."

Ben chuckled. "The last time I saw her she was weeding the garden."

Kirk nodded. "Thanks for the heads-up."

He scowled as he cleaned up after a hard day's work. They'd been together for lunch. It would have been nice if someone had let him know they all had plans tonight. Now he didn't know if he should just drive to town, grab a burger and stay at his house. Maybe he should run over to the garden and nonchalantly ask Callie if she wanted him to pick her up something, as well.

He'd just stay home and eat what they had in the kitchen, but he and Ben didn't really keep food at their house. Some crackers. A little peanut butter. Enough for midnight snacks.

He blew out an exaggerated breath as he put on clean clothes. *God, I'll just ask if she wants me to grab anything for her. No other questions. No pressure.* Praying for help not to revert back to his natural instincts of blowing a gasket if she made him mad, he walked to the main house.

As Ben said, Callie was in the back pulling weeds from the family garden. A big blue sun hat flopped on her head like an oversize Kentucky Derby hat. She wore black running shorts and a neon-green T-shirt, which made the hat look even more ridiculous, and yet adorable all at the same time.

"Need some help?"

Callie turned at his question, and he noted the reason for the hat. Her cheeks and nose burned red as a ripened tomato. "Nope. I'm almost done. Potato soup is hot on the stove."

"That was nice of you. I was gonna offer to pick us up a bite to eat."

She swatted the air. "No need for that. It's ready."

"Okay. I'll go spoon up a couple bowls."

She looked up at him, studying him for what seemed several minutes. Finally nodding, she said, "'Kay. I'll be there in a sec."

Kirk walked into the house, pulled out two bowls and filled them with soup. He took some crackers from the cabinet and the homemade pimiento cheese from the refrigerator. Spying some leftover baked beans in a plastic container, he nuked them in the microwave. It was a hodgepodge meal, to be sure, but it would suffice.

Callie avoided his gaze as she walked into the house and made her way to the sink. She'd taken off the hat and much of her hair stayed plastered to her head with electrically charged hairs sticking out from various angles. He prayed not to laugh at her and for God's wisdom on what to say as she washed her hands. Having a seat at the table, he waited for her to join him.

She sat across from him then traced her fingers through her hair. "I look a mess."

"You look like you've worked hard." He pointed to her face. "Sunburn to prove it."

"It was such a nice day. I wanted to be out in it."

She averted her gaze again, and Kirk placed his hands on the table but didn't reach for her. "Mind if I say grace? I'm starving."

She nodded. He didn't mind when she didn't take his hands. He hadn't expected her to. Finished with the prayer, he grabbed a spoon and dumped a heaping of baked beans on his plate, while Callie slathered pimiento cheese on crackers.

"Your mom makes the best pimiento cheese."

He nodded. "Gotta agree with you about that."

"I'm glad she's moving around a bit more."

"Me, too, and I know she's glad."

"Your dad's been worried sick."

"Yep."

The small talk ended, and silence covered them, but Kirk didn't mind. Her kiss had been his breaking point, forcing him to his knees. And God had given him peace.

"You're not still mad at me?"

Callie's voice held little more than a whisper, and Kirk swallowed his bite of potato soup and looked at her until she made eye contact with him. "Not at all."

"But after I… And I shouldn't have… And then I said…"

Kirk begged God for wisdom. If he were upfront, he'd tell her he loved her. Had always loved her. That before he hadn't understood what that meant, but now he would wait. With God's strength. The timing wasn't right to blurt out what he felt. She needed space and time to heal. He lifted his hand. "Really. It's okay."

She narrowed her gaze and cocked her head. "You're different."

He chuckled. "Been spending a lot of time with God."

Callie nodded. "That's good. Me, too." She placed her hand against her chest. "I'm healing. I know I am. But I'm afraid of loving again. Loving hurts."

Tears welled in her eyes, and Kirk longed to reach across the table and brush them away, to take her in his arms and promise he'd never allow another moment of pain in her life. But he couldn't do that, and he knew the Spirit prompted him to wait.

"You're right. It does hurt."

She studied him a bit longer then clasped her hands and placed them on the table. "I'm enjoying spending time with Princess again."

He nodded. "I'm sure she enjoys it, as well."

"You wanna go pick strawberries with me after we eat? They're almost all picked over, but I'm sure we can still find several."

Kirk's heart swelled in his chest. He would enjoy nothing more than to spend time with Callie. "Absolutely."

"We'll make Pamela fix a strawberry pie for tomorrow."

He rubbed his belly. "Best pie ever."

"I know." She twisted her mouth as she bit the inside of her cheek. "She's gonna have to teach me how to make it."

So that one day you can make it for our family. He didn't say the words, but he felt them in his heart. *Patience, Lord. Keep filling me up.*

Callie marveled at the change in Kirk the past few weeks. She kissed him, told him she hadn't meant it, he'd become angry initially, then it was as if he did a one-eighty. A complete change.

He didn't pester her for more information. He didn't pressure her to begin their relationship again. He was just there. Part of the family who was trying to love her back to wholeness.

Some days she felt herself again. She laughed as she played on the play area with Emma and Emmy. Devoured the summer wind whipping through her hair as they raced to see whose swing could go the highest. Her heart filled with new excitement for Pamela when they filled out her college application and applied for financial aid. Contentment wrapped around her when she fixed meals with Tammie then served their guests or helped customers at the gift shop or guided families through the play area and petting zoo. And nothing beat riding Princess out to the pond and spending time with the Lord as she fished or simply sat basking in the glory of God's creation.

Then she had dark moments when death seemed to grip her around the neck, threatening to steal her breath and life. She tried to work through those moments, to throw herself into the garden or the house or the shop. She'd pray and feel God's nudging of freedom and peace, but some days the grip was simply too tight. Today had been a battle.

Placing a strawberry in the third basket they'd filled, she sat on the ground. "Today's the anniversary."

Kirk stopped picking fruit and sat a little ways across from her. "Anniversary for what?"

She crossed her arms. "Dad's death."

"I'm sorry, Callie."

He didn't move toward her, and she appreciated

that. She didn't want his embrace. "It was a small service. Just me, his brother and Bill and his wife." Callie glanced at Kirk and pointed to her chest. "Who was not me."

His mouth drew up into a slow grin. "So I've heard."

"It was a couple days later the lawyer told us about the will." She huffed. "At least I didn't have to pay for the funeral."

She grimaced and peeked at Kirk. Bitterness sounded ugly when it slipped through her lips, and she felt mean and petty for being upset over her dad leaving everything to his brother and Bill.

Kirk's expression didn't change. She saw no traces of condemnation or repulsion at her attitude. He simply listened, and she found herself wanting to share more. She picked a ripe strawberry from the bush beside her and tossed it in the basket. "It's ironic that I get more upset about the anniversary of my dad's death than I do my mom's. She and I were so close."

"Unfinished business between you and your dad."

Callie nodded. "I suppose." She frowned and chewed on the inside of her cheek. "But I thought we had finished it. Made amends." She wrinkled her nose. "Then he left everything to them." Placing her hand against her chest, she shook her head at Kirk, imploring him to believe her. "I don't even want it. Don't need it. Yet, it bothers me."

"Acceptance."

She pondered the word. "Yeah. That's it. He died, and I thought he had accepted me. That he wished he'd never left."

She bit back the tears that threatened to spill down her cheeks. She didn't understand the man who fathered her, who had given her half her genes. He'd loved her mom. She knew he had. And she was his daughter. All those years, growing up, she'd thought she had been his little angel, the apple of his eye. She didn't understand. And she couldn't even confront him about what he'd chosen.

God, You have got to take away this pain. Take this hurt.

"I'm not going to say it's okay what he did. It makes me mad that he hurt you."

Callie swiped her eyes with the back of her hand. She looked at Kirk, waited for him to ask her to say more or tell her not to worry about it or to discount all she'd said in some way.

But he didn't.

She looked up at the heavens, wondering where her father was. Growing up, she'd always believed him a man of God. He'd gone to church with the family every Sunday. He'd provided for them all those years, but when hard times came, he'd left.

When she cared for him at the end, she'd asked him over and over where he stood with God. Most often, he changed the subject or patted her head and told her he was fine. The thought of the possibility that he'd never accepted Jesus into his life squeezed her heart with such fierceness she had to suck in a breath.

Tears pooled in her eyes and streamed down her cheeks before she had time to try to hold them back. A sob escaped her chest, and she covered her mouth with her hand.

Kirk moved closer and wrapped his arms around her. She didn't fight him. She needed the embrace now. The pain, the uncertainty were too much to face alone.

Burying her face in his shirt, she tucked her hands and arms against her chest but accepted his comfort. She felt small in his arms, like he could wrap her up and protect her from the pain. He didn't say anything, didn't shush her. He simply held her tight, and she allowed the release of her emotions. She didn't run away.

When she'd cried all she could, not a sniffle left in her body, Kirk let her go. She felt weak without his arms around her and surprised at how much she wanted them back. Kirk leaned over and she sucked in her breath. Surely, he wouldn't try to kiss her. She didn't want to be kissed. She wanted…

He placed a quick, chaste kiss on the top of her head then stood. "Think I'll leave you alone for a bit. If you need anything I'll be at my house."

Callie watched as he made long strides back to his place. She knew he loved her, and she loved him.

The admission of it hurt all the way to the tips of her toes. Love hurt. It came with joy, but it also came with pain. And for too long, pain had been the biggest participant in her life.

God, I can't give my heart to Kirk until You take this pain from me. I gotta get over my dad first.

And who's holding on to that hurt?

Callie swallowed the truth that she was the one holding the hurt. She knew that. She also knew that bad days were a reality when someone lost a loved one. How many times had she said those very words to the families of her patients?

Time is a terrific healer. She'd heard herself utter those words more times than she could count.

Just hold tight to each other. She squeezed her eyes shut when she thought of the additional advice she always gave. To hold tight to those they loved. To find strength from them.

She watched as Kirk walked into his house. She'd felt strength in his embrace. Semblances of peace weeded through her heart as she allowed him to hold her tight. *God, I know real healing comes only from You. But, I also know You use people to help us along.*

She stood, grabbed the basket handles and walked back to the main house. Once she cleaned the strawberries, she'd head to her room and spend some time alone with God. He'd never failed to show His will through the Word when her heart was willing to hear. And right now, she was willing.

Chapter 10

The month of June seemed to race by. Callie made it through the anniversary of her dad's death, as well as birthdays for both Emma and Emmy. The girls' birthdays were only one year and one day apart. Callie couldn't imagine what it must have been like for Pamela when Emmy was first born. Two in diapers. One toddling and making messes. The other totally dependent, needing bottle feedings and making different kinds of messes. Though it sounded overwhelming, Callie thrilled at the idea of attempting the challenge.

With Pamela's birthday only two days away, she and Tammie decided they'd take her to lunch, shop for some supplies for college in the fall and maybe splurge on a little pampering.

"But school doesn't start for over a month," whined Pamela.

Callie slipped into her flip-flops. "I know but it's your birthday, and we want to treat you to some fun."

"If I can make it in a cast," Tammie pointed to her foot, "you can go, too."

"See, we're making Mom get out and do things when she should be resting," said Pamela, pointing to her mother's bright green cast-covered foot.

Callie frowned. "Do you really not want to go?"

"She wants to go," said Tammie. "She's just a chicken about getting her hair cut."

Pamela gasped and grabbed her hair. "I'm cutting my hair?"

Callie laughed as she pushed Pamela into the car. They headed to the salon first. Pamela wiggled in the seat when Callie parked, but Callie opened the door and pulled Pamela out. "You're going to have a blast. I promise."

Tammie grabbed her crutches and hobbled toward the salon. "Don't worry, Pamela. We're all getting haircuts."

Callie lifted her shoulders and clapped. "I love a little pampering."

Pamela offered a weak smile, and Callie wrapped her hand through the crook of the birthday girl's elbow. "Come on. You're going to have a great time. No second thoughts allowed."

"I don't remember having first thoughts about getting my hair cut."

Callie tilted her head back and laughed. "Which is why you have no reason to have second thoughts."

Pamela grumbled as she walked into the salon. After signing in, the stylists sat them in a row of three chairs with Pamela in the middle. The dark-haired stylist with a pixie cut stood beside Callie. Callie lifted the tips of her hair. "I like to be able to wear a ponytail, but it needs some life."

The stylist nodded. "Maybe some layers. What about bangs?"

Callie glanced at Pamela, who looked as if she'd transformed into four-legged game locked in the glare of a car's headlights. Callie winked. "You want to? Might be fun."

Pamela released a sigh. "Okay," she said to her stylist, a young black woman with gorgeous waist-length dreads. She pointed at Callie. "Do whatever she's doing."

Callie closed her eyes as the young woman washed her hair. She relished the scratch of the stylist's fingernails against her scalp and neck. Her mind wandered to Kirk. The past few weeks had been wonderful. They worked well together whenever their paths crossed. She'd even gone fishing with Princess one morning, and Kirk was already at the pond when she arrived. Tempted to turn around and go back, she'd decided to stay, and they'd had a great time. Comfortable. Easy. He hadn't pressured her at all.

Once their hair had been blown dry, Callie bit back a chuckle at the panicked expression on Pamela's face as the stylist clipped away with a pair of scissors. Tammie hadn't opted for any changes in style and finished quicker than Callie and Pamela. The stylists lifted flat iron straighteners to their new bangs at the same time, and Callie couldn't help but wonder what Kirk would think of her new 'do.

With the styling complete, she ran her fingers through her locks. She liked the bangs. They gave her long blond hair a bit of sass. "What do you think, Pamela?"

Pamela turned her head left and then right. She bit her

bottom lip. "I can't believe I'm saying this." She looked up at the stylist. "But I love it."

The woman clicked her tongue. "The bangs look great on you." She touched Pamela's cheek with the back of her hand. "They accentuate those gorgeous cheekbones."

Tammie clapped. "I agree. You girls look terrific."

After paying for the haircuts, they drove to Pamela's favorite steakhouse. Tammie looked tired, and Callie wondered how she would make it through a trip to the mall, as well. Callie had tried to tell Tammie it would be too much for one day, but she had been adamant and Callie had given up arguing with her.

They walked inside and spied Mike sitting in a booth in the corner. A huge smile wrapped his face. "Don't you all look beautiful. I love the new 'dos. Isn't that what they're called?"

The women laughed as Tammie slipped into the booth beside Mike, and Callie and Pamela sat down across from them. Tammie pushed an envelope into Callie's hand. "Take her to the mall. Get her an outfit. Don't let her say no."

Pamela placed her hand on her chest. "Mom, I'm right here. You already bought me a haircut. We'll go home."

Tammie shook her head. "I knew you'd say that, which is why I had your dad meet us here. He's going to take me home, and the two of you are going shopping."

"But?"

"No buts, Pamela. I want you to come home with a new outfit."

Callie wrinkled her nose as she looked at the girl who was the closest she'd ever had to a sister. "And I'm buying you a book bag for school. So we have to go."

"Callie, don't be silly."

"I'm not being silly. Trust me. It may be a community college, but you'll need a backpack." She patted the top of Pamela's hand. "You'll thank me later."

"I mean—"

Callie nudged Pamela's elbow. "I know what you mean, but I'm getting you one, anyway."

Pamela relented, and they enjoyed lunch. By the time they'd finished, Tammie's discomfort had become evident. Mike insisted on footing the bill, and Callie and Pamela headed to the mall.

"This really isn't necessary," said Pamela.

Callie winked. "But it's been a lot of fun."

Pamela grinned. "It has been fun." She leaned back against the seat. "And I probably need it."

"You definitely need it."

Pamela didn't speak for a moment, and Callie wondered if the activity of the day was overwhelming her friend. "He still calls me sometimes."

"Who?"

"Jack."

Callie opened her mouth to respond, but nothing came out. She had no idea. The guy had been gone for, what did they say, since before Emmy's birth, so over five years.

She continued. "He doesn't say anything. Just hangs up."

"How do you know it's him?"

"He responded to Kirk one time, and Kirk recognized his voice."

Callie nodded. She had no idea what to say. From all she'd heard, Jack had behaved horribly the past few months he'd been around. Drinking all the time. Saying things to hurt Pamela. Even acted as if he'd hit her the night she kicked him out.

"Sometimes I think I still love him. How dumb is that?"

"Not dumb..." Callie's words trailed off. What should she say? Foolish, maybe. Not safe, probably. But the heart was such a hard thing to understand.

Pamela chuckled, a bitter sound, not of laughter but of sadness. "We Jacobs are a loyal lot. We fall in love, and it's forever."

Callie knew the words were directed to her. She had no doubt Kirk still loved her. If he confessed the truth with words, she wasn't sure how she'd react. Every day they grew closer. One day she believed she could respond by saying the words back to him, but was she ready now?

"Is Jack still drinking?"

Pamela nodded. "I think so."

"What would you do if he tried to come back?"

"Tell him to go back to wherever he's been."

Callie pulled into the mall's parking lot, found a spot, then turned off the car. She looked at Pamela. "You're a strong woman."

"Not really." She glanced back at Callie. "I serve a strong God."

Callie watched as Pamela pulled down the visor mirror and primped her hair. "Feels good to have a haircut."

Callie nodded. "I always think so."

She shut the visor. "Today's a good day to move on. Let's go buy me an outfit." She patted her purse. "I've got a little cash. Maybe we'll buy two."

Callie slipped out of the car and followed Pamela into the department store. It was a good day to move on. To allow God to clip off the pain that weighed her down. She needed a new outfit, as well. One that came white as snow and ready to allow love back into her heart. *God, it's a good day to move on.*

Kirk pressed the phone to his ear as he tried to make out Heather's words through her cries. He understood, and his heart sank. "Heather, I'm so sorry. Let us know how we can help."

He got off the phone, and his mother pressed her hand against his arm. "What is it? What happened?"

Kirk looked around the room. His parents, his sister and brother, his nieces and Callie all waited for him to share the news. Dread wrapped around him as he studied Callie. She'd come so far in healing since she'd come back to Bloom Hollow, back to his family. But there would always be sadness and tragedy in the world. It was an imperfect place with imperfect people.

He looked back at his mother. "Zack and Greta were in an accident." He swallowed the knot in his throat as his gaze found Callie again. "She didn't make it."

Dad shook his head and placed his hand on Mom's shoulder as she began to cry. Ben wrapped his arms around Pamela while Callie walked out the back door. Kirk took a step to follow her when Emma grabbed his hand. "I don't get it."

"What happened?" asked Emmy, as her bottom lip quivered. "Why is Mommy and Grandma crying?"

He knelt down and pulled both of them close. "There was a car accident, and a lady was hurt so bad that she passed away."

"What was her name?" asked Emma.

"Greta."

"From children's church?" said Emmy.

Kirk furrowed his brows. He hadn't realized Greta helped with the children at church, but it made sense. In fact, now that he thought about it, he had seen her in the back of the church, motioning for the children to go with her when the service called for children's church dismissal. "Yes, Greta, who helped in children's church," he answered.

Both girls swiped away tears with the backs of their hands. "Uncle Kirk, what does pass away mean?"

Kirk swallowed. They didn't understand, but how could they? Their small community had suffered hardly any deaths in the girls' few short years of life. The last funeral he'd been to had been Callie's mom's. His heart ripped at the thought of Callie going to her dad's funeral alone.

He looked back down at his nieces. "It means she died."

"She died?" said Emmy.

Crocodile tears flowed down Emma's cheeks. "Is she with Jesus?"

"Yes."

"Then why are we crying? Isn't she happy?"

"She is, but we won't get to see her anymore until it's time for us to go to Jesus."

Emmy's opened her eyes wide. "We won't see her in children's church?"

"No, she…"

Pamela grabbed both girls in a hug. "I'll explain it to them. Go talk to Callie."

He nodded and walked out the back door. He didn't see her. She couldn't have gone far. Her car was still in the driveway. He walked to the garden then realized she might have gone back to the cabin. He knocked on the door. She didn't answer. But then, he knew she might not answer if she didn't want to talk.

He looked at the barn and smacked his palm against his forehead. He knew where she was. Once at the barn, he saw that Princess was gone, as he'd expected. He saddled Thunder and rode out to the pond.

From a good distance, he could see them. Princess was tied to a tree, and Callie stood in front of her rubbing the horse's nose. He guided Thunder toward them. Callie didn't look up when he eased off the horse just feet away. He tied Thunder to the tree then took a step toward Callie.

"You know, death really is just a part of life," she said.

He stopped, praying for God to give him the right words. He knew Zack had to be hurting. If Callie had been in the wreck, Kirk would be reeling, begging God to explain why He took the woman he loved. The thought of it tightened his stomach and bile rose in his throat. He cleared his throat. "That's true, but sometimes we feel like it comes too soon."

Callie glared at him. "It's God's will. Are you arguing against God's will?"

He shook his head. "Not for a moment. But sometimes we don't understand it, and what He allows to happen in this world hurts."

"Don't you believe He's sovereign?"

"Yes."

"So He allowed it?"

Kirk nodded.

Callie blew out a long breath. "I believe that, too. The Bible says it, so I believe it." Her lips lifted in a slight grin. "How many times did we say that at church growing up?"

Kirk offered a weak smile. "A lot."

"Greta said it, too." Callie turned back toward Princess. She held the bridle as she rubbed Princess's nose. "You know Greta and I were close when we were kids. Used to spend the night at each other's houses." She shrugged. "Then we went to middle school and ended up in different cliques. You know how that happens."

He knew. He and several friends parted ways once the sports craze hit. Some of his elementary school friends found love in computers and video games. Kirk didn't care about throwing balls around or playing with electronic gadgets. He enjoyed working on the farm.

"We all hung out some in high school, though. Remember the time that big group of us went sledding?"

Kirk smiled. A bunch of them had gotten together and headed to Mason's huge hill. Only problem was at the bottom of that hill was a creek. After a few too many times sledding, he and Callie ended up hitting that creek, breaking through the ice and getting drenched from the waist down. Kirk laughed. "Took hours for you and me to dry off in front of Mason's fireplace."

Callie added, "And I don't think his dad was very happy about sharing his clothes with you."

Kirk laughed. "No, he wasn't."

Callie sobered and turned away from him. "God says He'll be glorified in all things."

"Even this death."

Callie turned toward him. "I know. I've seen it a dozen times over. One of my patients would pass on, and God would use their death to bring children or siblings back together. And yet..."

"It's still hard."

"And we're still never ready."

Kirk looked at the pond. It was his favorite spot on the farm. One of peace and quiet, where he could kick off his boots, feel the firm earth beneath his feet while he held a fishing pole in his hands. He could bask in the song of the crickets and frogs and inhale the fresh scent of God's nature. He found refreshment and renewal here.

It was Callie's favorite, as well. First place she went to when sorrow called on the phone. He had to believe God could use this spot to heal her, as well.

"I'm glad I came back, Kirk. I missed your family. And you."

He swallowed. Everything in him wanted to shout from the mountain peaks that he'd never stopped loving her. But his spirit still nudged him to wait.

"I'll be able to go to Greta's funeral. Say goodbye. I'm glad for that, as well."

Kirk didn't move. He begged God for the words to say. How much. How little.

She grinned. "Aren't you going to say anything?"

"I'm glad you're back." The words slipped from his lips without hesitancy. He wanted to say more, but for now that was enough.

She nodded as she unhooked Princess from the tree. "I suppose we should go back and pass around a few hugs to the family. See if anyone needs anything."

He helped her climb into the saddle then hopped onto Thunder's back. He liked the way she'd said that, as if they were her family, too. Because they were, or they would be, as soon as she would have him.

Chapter 11

Many in the community still reeled from Greta's death, and Callie prayed for Zack daily as he tried to adjust to life without her. As expected, good things had come from the tragedy. Two people in the church received Jesus into their hearts, and some of Greta's extended family had reunited.

Callie slipped on her rhinestone-studded red flip-flops, then tied a matching fat red ribbon in her hair. She rarely wore lipstick, but she adored the community's Independence Day celebration, so she painted her lips bright red. Gazing at her reflection, she knew she looked cheesy, but she didn't care.

Their community needed uplifting, and the Fourth of July was the perfect day to experience it. She walked to the main house and opened the back door. Emma and Emmy squealed when they saw her. Emma pointed to her lips. "I want red, too!"

Callie pulled a clear, shiny lip gloss out of her purse. "How 'bout some shine for the two of you?"

Emmy nodded and puckered her lips while Callie applied the gloss.

Emma crossed her arms in front of her chest and harrumphed.

"Or none," said Pamela.

Emma dropped her hands and puckered her lips. Callie slathered on the gloss then winked at Emma. "You look beautiful, darling."

"What about me?" asked Emmy.

Callie tickled her belly. "Of course, you do, as well."

Pamela motioned to the door. "Come on, girls. We have to go."

Callie's chest tightened for her friend. Since Greta's death, Pamela's countenance had changed. She seemed to enjoy taking care of herself, fixing her hair and makeup, and she was ready to start college classes in the fall, but a hardness seemed to have set up in Pamela's heart.

Callie prayed for her. She knew bitterness all too well, and it always took more than a person wanted to give. Having upgraded to a walking cast, Tammie hobbled into the room with Mike a few steps behind her. "Ben has already left, so it will be just you and Kirk in the truck. Is that okay?"

"No problem."

Tammie kissed her forehead. "You look so cute, dear."

Callie's heart warmed. She felt so much a part of this family. More so than before she left. Nothing would make her run again.

Tammie pointed to the counter. "Mike, grab the cole

slaw and corn on the cob. Callie, you and Kirk will have to take the pies and cookies." She placed her finger on her mouth. "Pamela must have taken the chicken out to the car already."

Mike grabbed his dishes. "We got them." He motioned to the door. "We gotta go, or we'll miss the blessing, which means we'll be last in line for food."

"Oh, hush." Tammie swatted the air, but she hobbled to the door. "Kirk will be here in a sec. He had to go back to his house to pick up the soft drinks."

"You go on ahead. We'll meet you there." Callie picked up the pie and tray of cookies and walked to Kirk's truck. With the doors locked, she placed the dishes on the hood of the truck. She watched him walk out of the house with two twelve packs of soft drinks.

He looked adorable in his bright red polo shirt and blue jeans. He still wore his cowboy boots and his oversize belt buckle with two cows grazing in front of a barn and silo. The same one he'd worn in high school, and she couldn't deny she loved the old thing. Seeing him, gorgeous as ever, sent her knees to knocking, and Callie didn't know if she'd be able to keep her secret until the fireworks.

In too few strides, he covered the distance between them and placed the drinks in the truck bed on her side. He fished in his front jeans pocket for his keys and unlocked her door.

Callie shook her hands beside her legs and stomped her foot. "Oh, no, I can't take it."

He frowned. "Can't take what?"

"I can't wait until the fireworks."

His lips drew up into a slow grin that almost had her

pressing her own against them. "Well, Callie, it won't be but a few hours. I know you like to watch them—"

"No. I mean I can't wait to tell you."

"Tell me what?"

"I love you, Kirk."

He took a step back as confusion etched his brow. Okay, so that wasn't exactly the reaction she'd expected, but the blame couldn't fall on him, she'd spent her time trying to run away from him.

She clasped her hands in front of her waist. "You heard me. I love you."

"Callie." He grabbed her arms with both of his hands and stared into her eyes. "Did you say what I think you said?"

"For crying out loud, boy, how many times does a girl have to say it?" She wiggled free from his grip. "I love you. I wanted to wait until the fireworks, but I couldn't stand it. I had it all planned in my mind, but you just looked so cute in your red shirt walking toward me, that I—"

She realized he'd leaned down and his lips were mere inches from hers. She placed her finger on his mouth. "Now that can wait. I already ruined it by telling you before we even ate dinner. I want our first kiss since I came back to be during the fireworks."

He grinned. "But our first kiss won't be at the fireworks."

"The last one doesn't count."

"Counted to me."

She rolled her eyes. "Okay, so it kinda counted to me, too. But I still want to wait until the fireworks."

"Only if you say it again."

"Say what?" She grinned, knowing exactly what he wanted.

"The three words I've waited over five years to hear again."

"I love you."

He touched the bottom of her ponytail and twirled her hair around his finger. "I love you, too, Cals."

Kirk watched as Callie filled her plate with a spoonful of each of the Fourth of July smorgasbord of food. She'd promised him a kiss during the fireworks, and he planned to find the perfect place for her to make good on her word.

He spied the old oak tree that sat to the side of City Hall. They'd shared many a quick kiss there during their high school years. It was the perfect place to hide from parents or nagging friends. *And it's just the right spot for tonight.*

Getting in the food line, he filled his plate and joined Callie and his parents in the lawn chairs they'd set up on the grassy area on the other side of City Hall. "Where is everyone?"

Tammie wiped her mouth with a napkin. "Haven't seen Ben since we got here, but Pamela took the girls to ride a couple of those carnival contraptions."

Kirk nodded, remembering the electric train, Ferris wheel and blow-up rides behind the stores on Main Street. In addition to the community potluck, people had put up vending carts of snow cones, kettle corn, cotton candy, fresh lemonade and more. Craft vendors, small business owners and various political candidates set up booths, as well.

His dad turned to him and said, "Son, Mom and I'll

need to take the truck before the fireworks so we can be sure to be back at the B and B before the guests' return."

"No problem." His dad handed him the car keys, and Kirk gave him the truck's. *So much for a quiet drive back to the farm.*

He wouldn't begrudge taking Pamela and his nieces home. Callie had promised him a kiss, and she'd told him she loved him. He itched to reach over and take her hand in his, but she'd just chomped into a cob of corn. Butter dripped from her fingers, even a bit from her chin. He chuckled as he took a napkin and wiped it off her face.

She grinned, exposing pieces of corn between her teeth. "Fanks."

He shook his head, and she wiped her mouth and hands then leaned close to him. "Still wanna kiss?"

"Yes."

She laughed as she picked up the corn again. Kirk bit into a piece of fried chicken and watched the people walking by. He spied Zack, his arm in a cast, walking by his parents. His hair had grown almost to his shoulders, and he was in desperate need of a shave. His clothes were rumpled, and Kirk wasn't sure he'd have recognized him if he weren't with his mom and dad. Kirk put down his plate and turned to his family. "Be right back."

He caught up with Zack and fell into step beside him. "How are you doing, man?"

"Horrible."

"But he's here," his mom said.

Zack looked at Kirk as he pointed to his chest. "Yes. I'm here."

There was no mistaking the sarcasm in his voice. His friend hurt, and Kirk couldn't blame him. "I'm really sorry."

Zack looked forward, staring past the crowd, the food, the vendors. "Me, too."

"I'm praying for you."

"I need it."

They turned on the side street leading to the rides and more vendors. Kirk didn't follow, but whispered another prayer of comfort for his friend.

Out of the corner of his eye, he saw Ben playing a ring toss game. His brother handed the man a couple of dollars, tossed the rings, lost and then handed him some money again. He walked to the booth. "Hey, Ben. Whatcha doin?"

Ben held the small ring between his pointer finger and thumb. He flicked it. The ring hit the top of a bottle then bounced onto the ground. Ben pointed to the cheap, overstuffed dog. "Gonna win that."

Ben handed the man another bill. It was the third time Kirk had seen him give the guy money. "Who you winning it for?"

Ben shrugged. "One of the girls, I guess."

Kirk grabbed his brother's arm. "Why don't you stop, man? Spend your money on something else."

Ben scowled. He pointed to his jeans pocket. "It ain't your money, so butt out."

Kirk raised his hands in surrender. "Fine. If you want to throw away your paycheck…"

"Maybe I do."

Disheartened, Kirk walked away from his brother. He knew Ben to be competitive, but he'd never before seen that look of pure determination. Sucking in a deep breath, he didn't have a clue what had come over his brother, but whatever it was wouldn't bother him today. Today was all celebration.

He started back toward Callie and his parents when someone grabbed his shirt. He turned and saw Emmy with Emma behind her. Pamela wore an exhausted expression. "I'm hungry. They want to play. If you go with them, they can have another half hour."

His sister had seemed angry and bitter lately. His mom asked him to pray for her, and he had been, but today he could see the frustration in her expression. He didn't know what was happening to his siblings.

Both girls clasped their hands and begged for him to allow them to play awhile longer. He couldn't resist his nieces. After a quick glance back at Callie, he was happy to see she seemed deep in conversation with his mother. He grabbed the girls' hands and headed back to the rides. "Thirty minutes. You got it?"

"Got it!" they yelled in unison.

Two hours later, Kirk dragged the girls to Pamela. They were hot and hungry, and he was exhausted from trying to keep up with both of them. Pamela took them to the picked-over tables, while Kirk plopped into the lawn chair beside Callie.

"Where's Mom and Dad?"

"They left." She pointed to the sky. "Almost dusk."

He picked up the soft drink he'd gotten several hours ago and took a long drink. Grimacing at the taste of the watered-down, syrupy liquid, he placed the cup back on the street.

"How 'bout this?"

Callie handed him a cup of fresh-squeezed lemonade. He took a long swallow. "Much better."

She chuckled. "Are you saying children wear you out?"

"Yes!"

She laughed again. "Well, it's a good thing I'm perfectly content to sit right here. What if I'd wanted to ride a few rides?"

Kirk lifted his hand. "Absolutely not."

After one more drink, he put the cup on the ground and took Callie's hand in his. She intertwined her fingers with his, and Kirk offered his thanks to God. Callie, his Cals, had come back to him within weeks of him surrendering his feelings for her to God. He couldn't be more thankful or filled up with praise.

Feeling refreshed, he stood and pulled up Callie. "You wanna take a walk?"

"What about the fireworks?"

"We'll still be able to see them."

Callie narrowed her gaze at him as if unsure she should trust him. "I suppose."

He held her hand in his. If it were up to him, he'd never let it go again. They walked past the crowd and toward the oak tree.

She smiled up at him. "I believe I know where we're going, and we won't have a very good view of the fireworks."

"Good enough for me."

"Me, too."

They reached the tree, and Kirk drew her into a quick hug. "I didn't know how long it would be until I would hear those words again."

She pointed to the ground. "Let's sit."

He felt like a heel. He should have brought the chairs or a blanket or something. He sat beside her and took her hand in his again.

"I'm a little surprised myself." She brushed back her bangs with her free hand. "I mean, I'd been praying and reading His Word, and I knew He wanted me to be free of the pain of the past. But when Greta died…" She shook her head and exhaled a deep breath. "I knew I didn't want to spend however much life I have left without love." She gazed at him. "Especially your love."

Kirk's heartbeat raced in his chest. His stomach churned as it did the first time he kissed her. He leaned forward. "Now?"

She nodded as she released his hand and placed both of her palms against his cheeks. Thrill shot through him when her lips touched his. He wrapped his arms around her and drew her closer. Her fingernails gently scratched his neck as she moved her hands into his hair.

Too long. It had been much too long since he'd felt her lips against his. Too long, and he had to pull away. He released her and grabbed her hand in his. "We need to watch the fireworks."

She giggled as she nestled closer to him and rested her head on his shoulder. "I love you, Kirk."

"I love you, too, Cals."

Chapter 12

According to Mike and Tammie, Jacobs Family Farm had more customers during the month of July than they'd ever had in the history of their family business. And Callie felt every moment of it. She'd cleaned bedrooms and bathrooms, sold crafts and snacks, baked desserts and made lunches, played on the play area and fed animals. Not to mention the work in the yard, the garden, the orchard, and trying to keep her little cabin clean.

"So, you and Kirk have a hot date tonight, huh?" said Ben as he walked into the kitchen of the B and B, opened the refrigerator and grabbed a soft drink.

"Just dinner and a movie, but the temperature is definitely warm enough to say it will be a hot date." She winked, and Ben shook his head.

"I'm glad the two of you are back together."

"So am I."

Emmy held up a bottle of lime-green nail polish. "We're going to paint her toenails."

Ben lifted his brows, and Callie held up the pink bottle. "This color."

"But you're going to do mine in purple, right?" said Emma.

"Absolutely."

Ben sat at the table across from Callie. "Where is Pamela, anyway?"

"She went to campus to pick up a school book she couldn't order online."

"I can't believe her classes start a whole week before mine."

"When is Kirk taking you to the university?

"Next Wednesday."

Emma wrapped her arms around Ben's waist. "I don't want you to leave. Who's going to help me with my math?"

Ben rubbed her head with his knuckles. "I'm sure someone will be able to help you."

"Second grade math is hard."

Callie bit back a chuckle. "But your mommy's good at math. She'll be able to help you."

Emmy twisted the polish bottle then pulled out the brush. "Can I paint your toes, Uncle Ben?"

"No, pumpkin, you can't." Ben hopped out of the chair. "On that note, I'm out of here."

Callie giggled as Ben exited the house with a swiftness she'd rarely seen from him. She looked at Emmy. "Guess he doesn't like toenail polish."

Emma cackled. "Well, he is a boy, silly."

"That he is." Callie took the bottle from Emmy. "Hand me your foot, and I'll paint those tootsies."

Emmy smiled as she lifted her foot onto Callie's lap. Callie painted the lime-green color on the girl's toes then added small pink dots. Emmy squealed with delight and ran into the living room to show her grandpa before Callie could remind her to be careful. She painted Emma's toes purple with pink dots, and the child followed her sister racing into the living room to show off her polish.

She heard the music from the girls' favorite cartoon coming from the living area. They must have convinced their grandfather to switch stations. She looked down at her bare toenails. "Guess I'm on my own."

Filing the nails, her mind wandered to her date with Kirk that night. It had been so long since she'd been on a real date. Kirk, as excited as she, said he would pick her up in his truck at six o'clock sharp. They could have easily met here at the house, but he wouldn't hear any of it. He'd grumbled when she'd suggested as much. "It's our first real date since you've been back. We're doing it right."

She folded her leg until her knee met her chest and her foot rested on the chair. With careful strokes, she applied the pink polish then switched legs and repeated the process.

Glancing at the clock, she realized painting the girls' nails and her own had taken longer than she expected. She needed to get ready. Walking on the balls of her feet, she made her way back to the cabin. She opened the screen then pushed open the door. Still balancing on her heels, she stepped on a small rock and lost her balance.

Trying to keep her toes from getting ruined, she stepped back on her foot and reached for the screen door with both hands. Her right hand caught air, but her left hand caught the door. She yanked forward and crashed into the side of the door.

She touched the side of her chest then worked down to her hip. "Ouch. That really hurt."

Still on the balls of her feet, she carefully made her way into the house. Her left side throbbed. She walked into the bedroom and took off her shirt. The door left an angry red imprint all the way down. With cautious fingers, she pressed along the line. Her abdomen seemed fine, probably just a bruise, but the side of her chest seemed a little swollen.

Was the swelling due to hitting the door, or was there a lump there? A wave of panic laced through her as she thought of her mom battling breast cancer. Blinking several times, she sighed at her inner dramatics. "When a person falls and bruises a part of her body, the area often swells a bit."

She threw the shirt in the hamper then walked to her closet to take down the bright pink sundress she'd chosen to wear on the date.

Fear niggled the back of her mind, and she took another deep breath, as the urge to feel the spot again welled inside her. "Callie Dawson, you are a nurse. You know that chances are the swelling is nothing but the injury," she scolded herself aloud.

But chances sometimes go the other way. She felt the side of her chest again. Definitely not normal. She tried lifting her hands above her head to see if she could detect anything obvious. Lowering her arms, she fumed at herself. *Just because my mother had breast cancer does not mean I will get breast cancer.*

Annoyed, she pressed her palms against the dresser top and read the verse she'd printed and taped on the mirror several months ago. "'The Lord is good.'" She spoke the words aloud, forcing them to sink into her anxious mind. "'A refuge in times of trouble. He cares for those who trust Him.'"

She spoke to her reflection. "He's good. He cares for me. No matter what."

Her mind shifted to her mother and how much she loved the Lord, to Greta and how Greta loved and served Him. God being good, and God caring for her, had nothing to do with Him allowing bad things to come into her life. She knew that. The swelling could mean bad news. It could be more than a bruise.

However, I did just ram my whole body into the side of a door, so most likely, it's simply a bruise.

Callie laughed out loud. She was excited about the date, but she was obviously anxious, as well, because she was making a great big disease out of a little bitty bruise.

Making her way into the bathroom, she brushed her teeth then plugged in the flat iron. She freshened her makeup then fixed her hair. After applying hairspray and then perfume, she put on the sundress. She slipped on the rhinestone sandals she'd bought on the birthday mall trip with Pamela. She fastened the straps then stood to her full height and looked at herself in the mirror.

She hadn't dressed up for a date in years. It felt good. She looked pretty. For a moment, she wished her mom was in the other room, waiting for her to come out of the bathroom. Mom would gush over how beautiful her girl was.

God, I suppose I'll always miss her. She put on the small diamond heart necklace her mother always wore. Smiling at her reflection, she touched the charm. *But I have a memory of her right here.*

* * *

Kirk placed his hand on the small of Callie's back and guided her into the Italian restaurant. The menu was definitely not his favorite, but he wanted tonight to be perfect. He pulled out her chair then sat across from her.

She leaned forward. "We didn't have to come here."

"Why? Do you not like it anymore? It used to be your favorite."

"It is my favorite, but I know it's not yours."

He grinned. "I guess we both remember a lot about each other."

She cocked her head and narrowed her gaze. "Bet I remember more."

Before he could respond, the waiter arrived at their table. The teenage redhead placed a drink napkin in front of each of them. "What can I get you two to drink?"

Kirk lifted his eyebrows. "She'll have a raspberry Italian soda."

Callie dipped her chin in affirmation. She pointed toward him and said, "And he will have a diet Coke with no ice."

The waiter nodded then walked away, promising to take their orders when he returned.

"Good job." Kirk clasped his hands on top of the table. "Do you remember my favorite color?"

"Green. Mine?"

He lifted his finger. "Lime-green. Food?"

"Steak and baked potato, extra butter, no sour cream."

"Spaghetti with tomato sauce."

"Marinara."

"Same thing."

"True." She placed her elbows on the table and rested her chin on her fists. "Season?"

"Fall, when the leaves change."

"Spring, because you can get your hands in the dirt again."

Kirk grinned. "Sports?"

She wrinkled her nose. "None. Unless farming is a sport."

"None for you, either."

"Kids?"

He lifted two fingers.

She raised both hands. "As many as you have fingers, which the thought of always made me cringe a little. I mean somebody's gotta give birth to that brood."

He leaned back in his seat and laughed. The waiter showed up with their drinks and took their orders. True to their preferences, he ordered the only steak on the menu, while Callie ordered spaghetti and meatballs with marinara sauce.

Callie wrapped the straw between her thumb and finger and took a drink. "So, what movie are we going to see?"

Kirk dropped his hands beneath the table and wrung them together. What to tell her? He didn't want to ruin the surprise, but he couldn't lie to her, either. "I think we'll skip a movie. I have something else planned."

She leaned forward. "Bowling?"

He shook his head as he envisioned falling on his face because he tried to release the ball but his fingers were stuck in those little holes.

"Skating?"

He stared at her, and she exploded in laughter. He cleared his throat. "Are you laughing because you believe I can't skate? I'll have you know..."

She gripped the side of the table. "Since when can you skate?"

"Since never."

"So, where are we going?"

"It's a surprise."

Her eyes lit up. "I love surprises, and I love to try to figure them out."

"I know." He wiped his hands on the sides of his pants. "I know you quite well, remember?"

The food arrived, saving him from the third degree he knew she was about to give him. He offered a prayer over their food then lifted a silent prayer for God to help him make the night perfect.

She was quiet through dinner, and Kirk knew she contemplated what he had planned for the date. He wished the woman would sit back and enjoy their time together. But she wouldn't. She wanted to know everything, and he loved her, anyway.

"Are we going to the high-school football game?"

He scrunched his face. "What?"

"I didn't think so. It's too late to go hiking, and I…"

"Would you just enjoy eating your dinner?"

She bantered back and forth with him through the rest of dinner. The waiter arrived with the check just before he blurted out the plans simply to get her to stop guessing.

He opened the passenger's door to the cab of the truck and helped her climb inside then ran around and hopped into his seat. He headed back toward the farm.

"This was my next guess."

"What?"

"The pond." Her words came out little over a whisper, and he wondered if she'd figured it out.

Well, even if she had, he had a few other surprises for her. Things he hoped she wouldn't have thought about. He pulled onto the old dirt road he and his dad and brother had worn out on their many trips to the pond. His heartbeat raced as he drew nearer to the destination. His hands started to sweat and he wiped them one at a time on his pants.

Callie inched closer to him and rested her head on his shoulder. Courage swelled within him. He could do this. It was what he wanted, and no matter what she said, he had to ask.

He saw the pond in the distance and drove toward the single light on the linen-covered table that he'd had his mom and dad bring out to the pond. Callie raised her head and pointed. "What is that?"

"You'll see."

He drove a little farther, then stopped the truck, got out and helped her out of the cab. Taking her hand in his, he walked her toward the table. His parents had turned on a small battery-operated lamp, as he'd asked. Beside it was the dozen long-stemmed red roses he'd ordered. On the ground was a small cooler.

He offered Callie a chair. She hadn't said a word, but kept her fingers pressed against her lips. Opening the cooler, he lifted out two soft drinks and two pieces of cake. He placed one of each in front of Callie. "Dark chocolate cake with milk chocolate icing is still your favorite?"

Callie nodded.

He bent down and lifted out a plastic container of raspberries. He placed three on the top of her cake. "Raspberries are still your fruit of choice?"

She nodded.

"And the number three is your favorite?"

She nodded again.

He took her hand in his and allowed his thumb to trace its softness while he begged God to still his pounding heart. "For as long as I live, I don't think I'll ever be able to forget a thing about you."

With his free hand, he pointed to his temple. "You're ingrained in my head." Then he tapped his chest. "And my heart. I love you with all that is in me."

He reached into his pants pocket and pulled out the black box. He popped open the lid and turned it to face her. "Do you remember this ring?"

Callie gasped and touched the tip of the diamond with her fingertip. She nodded. "It's the one I picked out years ago."

"I bought it. Before I asked for the break, I bought it. I think it's what scared me. I loved you with everything in me, but the thought of getting married seemed impossible to my young mind. When you left, I looked at it every day for months. Furious with myself that I let someone else have you."

"Oh, Kirk."

"I kept it because I knew I'd always love you." He got out of his chair and knelt in front of her. "Cals, I'm never going to let you go again. Please say you'll be my wife."

Callie wrapped her arms around his neck, and he pulled her close. She grimaced, and he let her go.

Tears streamed down her cheeks and she shook her hands. "Don't mind that. I ran into the door and bruised my side, but I want a hug. Just be easy."

He tried again and pressed his lips to hers. "You never answered me."

"My answer is yes. A thousand times yes."

"And let me guess. A fall wedding?"

"How'd you know?"

He kissed her nose, then her eyes, then her cheeks, then her lips. "Because Callie Dawson, I know you."

Chapter 13

Kirk walked up the concrete steps leading to the three arches in front of the Health Science Center at the University of Tennessee. He and Ben had walked all over the campus, checking out each building where Ben had, or believed he would have, a class.

He was happy for his brother, to be doing what he wanted to do, but Kirk didn't understand Ben's desire to leave the farm and come to a place of constant activity and noise. Sure, the farm had its fair share of customers, and Kirk fell asleep from sheer exhaustion the moment he closed his eyes at night. But he woke up to the sound of a rooster crowing and birds calling, not car horns blowing and machines chattering.

The University of Tennessee was pretty and all, had a lot of terrific design and landscaping, but there were no mountains, not even any rolling hills. It was as if they'd left Tennessee all together. Kirk wouldn't be able to breathe without nature around him, his animals, the orchard, the farm.

Pamela had started classes a week ago, and Kirk had been as thrilled for her as anyone. She'd been especially somber the past few months. Maybe getting her degree would be good for her. Make her feel as if she had a purpose, even though a piece of paper wouldn't give her value. She'd already been deemed special by the Lord. But maybe it was something she felt she had to do.

Besides, he wasn't against college. He'd gone to the community college Pamela now attended. Got his associate's degree in business and took a few agriculture classes, as well. He wanted to have the knowledge to use and care for the resources God had given him. But a degree in engineering, which was what Ben wanted, or accounting as Pamela desired. He wrinkled his nose. Nah. Those types of sit-in-the-office-all-day jobs weren't for him.

Kirk patted his brother's shoulder. "So, what do you think?

"I think I can't believe I didn't come here right out of high school."

Ben's gaze followed a group of girls that walked past them. One girl with long red hair turned around and smiled at Ben. Kirk nudged his little brother. "Remember, you're here to learn."

He meant it in jest, but Ben scowled. "I know why I'm here, but I plan to go on a few dates and have a little fun, as well."

Kirk crossed his arms in front of his chest. "I was only teasing you."

"Well, I'm tired of it. I'm not just the baby brother. I'm a grown man making my own decisions." He lifted his hand. "When you were my age, didn't you want to have some fun?"

"When I was your age, I had planned to ask Callie to marry me. Instead, I let her get away, and I lost five years with her."

Ben scoffed. "You really think you were ready for marriage at twenty?" He pointed to himself. "There's no way I'm ready to settle down." He opened his arms wide. "I want to get an education, meet new people and experience different things. I wouldn't want to be tied down to a woman."

"Evidently, you and I are very different."

"Come on, Kirk. If you and Callie had gotten married all those years ago, you probably would be miserable now. You each needed time to grow up."

Kirk hadn't thought about the good in their five-year separation. He'd been able to grow in his faith and learn to care for the family's land. He'd worked harder and longer than he would have if Callie had been home waiting for him. As a result, their family farm thrived.

And Callie. She probably would have never gotten her degree. She'd told him one day she wanted to work with hospice patients again. What a wonderful gift—to be able to give comfort to those who are dying. Plus she'd been there with her dad when he died. That wouldn't have happened if they'd been married. She still carried pain from her father, but at least she'd been there for him when he needed it. She had no regrets.

Kirk looked at his brother. "I think you're probably right, though I don't regret I'm marrying her now."

Ben's expression softened. "I'm happy for you two." He spread his arm toward the campus. "Hoping I'll meet a girl I'm as crazy about." He elbowed Kirk. "But not for a year or two."

Kirk shook his head. "Let's go see if the dorm is ready for us to unload your stuff."

They made their way back to the dorm parking lot. Many of the students had already moved in, but the waiting lines for the elevator snaked out the front door, so Kirk and Ben unloaded boxes out of the truck and packed them up the stairs to Ben's dorm.

Ben opened the door, only to be greeted by a short, small-framed guy with wire-rimmed glasses. "You must be Ben Jacobs." The guy's voice sounded like that of a twelve-year-old boy who hadn't yet made it to puberty.

Kirk put down the box he carried while Ben extended his hand. "I am."

"Let me get out of your way, so you can unpack." He pointed to bunk beds along the left wall. "I already took the top bunk. I don't weigh much so I figured I'd go ahead and take that one."

Ben nodded, and Kirk had to bite his lip to keep from laughing at the mental image of Ben scaling a wooden ladder every night to get to his top bunk. The room looked clean enough, but it was small. Kirk felt claustrophobic just standing in the hall looking into it.

He tallied the furniture. Bunk beds. Two desks and chairs. Two three-drawer dressers. That was it. And little room for anything else.

Ben glanced back at Kirk. "You wouldn't be able to do this, would you?"

"Nope."

Ben murmured, "Not sure I can, either."

Wanting to encourage his brother, Kirk hefted the box

and walked into the room. "Come on. You'll get used to it. In a week's time, you'll love it here."

As soon as the words left his mouth, Kirk knew they were true. He and Ben might have shared parents and the same DNA, but they were different as a tractor and a push mower. Kirk thrived on being in open spaces and working with his hands. Ben enjoyed being around people and working with his mind, conjuring the easiest, most efficient way to get something done. Kirk just threw himself into the work until it was finished.

A sudden sadness settled in his gut. Kirk would have the house all to himself. At least for the next couple months until he and Callie got hitched. Ben would always be his brother, but he realized chances were Ben would find his way somewhere in a city working an office job and living in an apartment not too much bigger than this dorm room.

Kirk wanted Ben to follow God's leading for his life, to use the talents God had given specifically to Ben, but he was gonna miss his brother, too.

The elevators either weren't working, moved slower than molasses or were packed to maximum capacity, so they walked back down six flights of stairs. Filling their arms with all that was left in the bed of the truck, they maneuvered back up the six flights. Ben's roommate still hadn't returned, so Kirk helped him make the bed and organize his stuff.

Mom would have been much better suited to help Ben unpack, but with each thing they took out of the box, Kirk found himself missing his brother a bit more. *I wonder if she sent me because she knew she'd be a blubbering mess by the time she left.*

With the last of his snacks packed into a plastic container and shoved under his bunk bed, Kirk knew it was time to say goodbye. Ben extended his hand, but Kirk grabbed him in a bear hug. "I'm going to miss you, little brother."

"I'll be back in a couple weeks for Labor Day."

"But it won't be the same."

Ben shook his head. "I suppose it won't."

"If you ever need anything, I'm just a phone call away."

Ben nodded, and Kirk gave him one last hug before he turned and walked out the door. Taking the steps two at a time, he wondered at the sadness in his gut. Ben had followed him around the farm for twenty years. It was time for him to set out on his own. Change was inevitable, but Kirk didn't have to like it.

October nineteenth. Only two months away. Callie's fingers tingled with excitement. She would have never imagined when she moved back to Bloom Hollow in May that in only six short months she'd become Mrs. Kirk Jacobs. She held back the giggle that rose in her chest. How many times in high school had she doodled that name on notebook paper, agenda books, even church bulletins?

"You ready to go inside?"

Tammie hooked her arm around Callie's elbow. She looked up at the bridal dress shop's sign, promising hundreds of styles to choose from. She nodded as Pamela opened the front door then they walked inside.

A tremble of thrill and trepidation washed over her when she realized the shop had not exaggerated. She'd never seen so much satin, lace and sequins, so many shades of white. A sudden shot of pain assaulted her heart as she thought of how much her mother would have enjoyed wedding dress shopping. *She always loved Kirk, too.*

Offering a quick prayer to help her relish the day, she glanced at Tammie who rummaged through racks of clear plastic covered dresses. Now free of her cast, she had no trouble oohing and aahing over the various styles. Thanksgiving joined the pain in her heart. Callie would miss her mom for the rest of her life, but God had given Callie a soon-to-be mother-in-law who loved her as if she were one of her own.

"This is gorgeous!" Pamela pointed to a Cinderella ball gown look-alike on a mannequin by one of the registers.

Callie twisted her mouth. "Definitely beautiful, but too big."

Pamela whooped. "And probably too expensive. This thing is over ten thousand dollars."

"Definitely too much."

Pamela let go of the price tag. "What is our budget?"

"Well..." Callie had thought about how much she wanted to spend on the wedding. She had a decent savings, but she wasn't sure she wanted to spend all of it on a one-day celebration.

Tammie lifted her hands. "We'll talk budget later. Mike and I are paying for the wedding."

Callie's jaw dropped. "What?" She shook her head. "No."

Tammie crossed her arms in front of her chest and raised her eyebrows. "Mike and I already discussed it. We are." She lifted one hand and pointed her finger. "In fact, we knew you would want to argue about it, so we decided that you and Kirk may pay for the rehearsal dinner, but that we would still pay for the wedding."

"What if we refuse?"

Tammie's expression fell, and she touched Callie's forearm. "Please don't. We've always thought of you as our own daughter, and we want to do this for both of you."

A sense of belonging settled in her heart. Though she hadn't realized it, hadn't given it a name, she'd longed for the feeling all those years she was away from Bloom Hollow. All the years since her mother died. She wrapped her arms around Tammie. "Thank you."

A catch sounded in Tammie's voice. "I should have never let you go."

Callie released her and thought of the conversation she and Kirk had when he returned from dropping off Ben at the university. The five years apart had been difficult, and when she thought about her dad, she still ached inside. But the separation had allowed both of them to grow into people who depended on the Lord and who were ready to be married to each other. Callie shook her head. "No. God used that time."

"May I help you ladies find something?" An older woman with a wide welcoming smile and gray hair stacked high on her head walked up to them. She looked from Callie to Pamela. "Who's the lucky lady?"

Pamela's expression drained of color as she pointed to Callie. Callie held out her left hand, and the woman complimented the square-cut Princess diamond set in a diamond-studded white-gold band. She'd stared at it constantly since he'd put the ring on her finger over a week ago. She never tired of looking at it.

The woman clapped then lifted both hands to her

mouth. "Well, I am Zella, and I will be happy to help you find the dress of your dreams. What is our price range?"

Tammie quoted a number that sent heat up Callie's spine. She turned toward her. "Tammie, that's too much."

Tammie lifted her hand. "What did we just agree to?"

Callie glanced at Pamela who shrugged.

"Wonderful. We have plenty to choose from in that price range. When is the wedding?"

"October," said Tammie.

Zella gasped and clapped her hands. "Two months. We'll need to get right on it." She addressed Callie. "So, what are you looking for?"

Callie shifted her weight from one foot to the other. Quite probably the only bride on the planet who hadn't scoured through magazines, she had no idea what she wanted in a dress.

Obviously noting the hesitancy, Zella asked, "Do you want white or ivory?"

That was easy. "White."

"Lace?"

"Yes."

"Pearls?"

Callie thought a moment then shook her head. She liked pearls but she didn't want to trip over them if they happened to come off the dress.

"Sequins?"

Callie shook her head.

"Rhinestones?"

"Maybe."

Zella clapped her hands together. "You're doing great. I'm forming a picture in my mind. Sleeves?"

Callie shook her head.

"So strapless?"

The thought of nothing holding up the dress made her stomach tighten with a moment of panic. "Well, maybe something."

Zella touched her shoulders. "A small strap off the shoulders maybe?"

Callie nodded. "That sounds pretty."

"And since it may be cool, how about some long satin gloves?"

Callie shrugged. She wasn't sure she'd like them but she wasn't exactly opposed to them, either.

Zella nodded. "Okay, so that's a maybe. What about the length? Long with a train?"

Callie smiled. At least she knew something she wanted. "Yes. Long with a long train."

"Good. Last thing. How about volume? Do you want a ball gown?" Zella opened her arms wide around her hips. "Or straight?" She brought her hands down, touching both of her hips.

Callie cocked her head. "Maybe somewhere in between."

Zella snapped her fingers. "I'll be back. I know the dress." She headed toward the other side of the store then turned and smiled. "And Mom, it is well within your price range."

Callie looked at Tammie, realizing she didn't mind Zella thought she was Callie's mother. Tammie wrapped one arm around her shoulder. "I can't wait to see it."

Zella called for them to join her in the dressing room. The dress looked beautiful on the hanger. Callie changed into the dress, and a slight groan escaped her lips when she hit the sore spot on the left side of her chest. The rest of her side had healed, but that spot remained stubborn. Probably didn't help that she kept pushing on it, fearing it was more than a bruise. Ignoring the discomfort, she called Zella into the dressing room to help lace up the back.

Even without a mirror, Callie knew it was lovely. She stepped out of the dressing area, and Pamela and Tammie gasped. Tears welled in Tammie's eyes and she covered her mouth with her hand. Callie looked at her reflection.

It was perfect. Everything Zella described. Small straps that fell off her shoulders connected to a tight corset that accented her curves without being distasteful. Small rhinestone designs covered the top right side of the corset as well as the bottom left. Below her waist, the satin dress puffed out just a bit, trailing all the way to the floor with the same rhinestone designs as on the corset splattered on the dress and train. The satin material gathered up on the right side, exposing soft white lace.

Zella hustled to the other side of the dressing room then returned with white gloves, a rhinestone tiara and a long veil. She shimmied the gloves all the way up to Callie's elbows then fixed the headpiece.

When she moved from in front of the mirror, Callie's heart squeezed with happiness and excitement. She extended both hands and twisted left to right. "Oh, Zella, it is perfect."

"Kirk will love it," said Pamela.

Tammie hopped up from her chair and kissed Callie's forehead. "Your mother would be so proud, just as I am."

"She would," Callie murmured. She studied the dress. "First dress I try on, and it's perfect." She turned toward Tammie and grinned. "Just like Kirk's my first love, and he's perfect for me, too."

Chapter 14

Kirk opened the door to the fast food restaurant, and Emma and Emmy walked inside. With Pamela attending morning classes, Kirk volunteered to take the girls to school. He'd wake up before the sun, take care of the animals then wash up before picking up the girls at the main house. They drove to a local fast food restaurant and enjoyed pancakes and sausage for breakfast, then he dropped them off at school.

As it turned out, he enjoyed the time with his nieces. With a steady flow of customers anxious to enjoy the farm before the weather turned cooler, he'd had little time in the evenings to spend with the girls. Not to mention, he didn't want to give up evening hours with Callie. Taking the girls to school proved the perfect solution.

They ordered their food, then Kirk picked up the tray and headed to the booth where they always sat. He handed the girls their food then offered a quick prayer of thanks.

Emmy opened her milk carton. "Uncle Kirk, I can write my name."

Kirk laughed. "You could write your name last year."

She nodded. "I know, but Ms. Cann says I have the best handwriting of anybody."

Emma rolled her eyes, and Kirk gave her a warning look not to start a fight with her sister.

"And Ms. Cann lets me sit by Anna. She's nice, but she's really quiet. I think Ms. Cann wants me to help her talk more."

Kirk chuckled. He had a feeling the teacher's intentions were directly the opposite.

"And yesterday," Emmy continued, "I got to do the weather chart, and since it was raining, I got to put the storm cloud on the chart. It's my favorite." She scrunched her nose. "But in real life, I like it better when it's sunny."

"Oh, for crying out loud." Emma sighed, sounding just like Pamela when she was frustrated.

Kirk studied his niece. She'd been exasperated a lot lately. He swallowed his bite of pancake. "How are things going for you, Emma?"

"Fine." She twirled the bottom of her ponytail, but she never looked up from her plate.

"You don't sound fine. What's wrong?"

She slumped back in the seat. "Momma said she'd braid my hair. She forgot. Again."

Emmy smacked her lips together. "Momma was gonna put my hair in piggy tails, but she forgot, but then Grandma said she'd do it. She said she'd do Emma's, too, but Emma said no." Emmy emphasized Emma's answer and shook her head back and forth.

Emma didn't respond. Pamela had been acting different since Greta's death. He remembered the day he'd heard Jack's voice over the phone. Maybe, it wasn't only Greta's death bothering his sister. His blood burned thinking about that man and how he'd chosen the bottle over his wife and daughters.

Emmy bit into her sausage patty. "Grandma says Momma is refreshed and we need to pray for her."

"Depressed, dummy," Emma mumbled.

"Don't call your sister names," he reprimanded Emma. He turned to Emmy. "And don't talk with your mouth full."

The girls finished their breakfast, while Kirk pondered what his mom had told the girls. He knew Pamela had been withdrawn, but she must be having a harder time than he realized if his mom and nieces had discussed it. Maybe, he should talk with Pamela later. Find out if Jack was still calling. Ask her what he could do to help. Maybe she needed some help with her jobs on the farm. Or she was struggling with some of her classes.

A tug pulled at his heart. He couldn't fix her. He knew that from what he had noticed. Knowing his mom, she'd already tried everything he could think of to help. The best thing he could do was pray for her.

God, I know prayer is a powerful thing, but for a guy who likes to dig in, get his hands dirty and finish the task, it's hard to talk to You and then wait for You to do Your thing. He inwardly sighed. Prayer and patience worked with Callie. It was probably true for Pamela, as well.

They collected their trash and dumped it in the can.

He walked them to the truck, helped them inside then buckled them into their seat belts. Once at the school, they hopped out of the truck.

Relief filled him when Emma perked up when she saw a little dark-haired girl with yellow bows in her hair. His older niece fell into step beside the girl. He could tell the two chatted as they walked toward their teacher.

Emmy spied Ms. Cann and lifted her hand high in the air in an exaggerated wave. She ran to the light-haired woman with short, choppy hair. He watched as the lady nodded her head while Emmy talked and talked. No telling what his younger niece was saying to the woman.

He chuckled as he pulled out of the drive. Though they came from the same parents, the girls were as different as night and day. He wondered what his and Callie's children would be like. Would they be dark haired like him and love farming and getting their hands dirty? Or would they be light haired and ready in a moment to help someone who was hurting? They'd probably be a combination of both, each taking different traits in different ways.

He thought of Callie's groaning when she relayed her remembrance that he wanted as many kids as he had fingers. He still did. As many as Callie was willing to have, he was willing to have. He wanted a whole houseful. As many boys as girls, if God allowed. He was ready to start now. Glancing out the windshield, his heart thrilled when he saw a lone tree boasting a few salmon-colored leaves. The wedding couldn't come soon enough.

Callie had dreaded this day. The feeling was nothing new. She'd never enjoyed going to the doctor for her yearly female exam, but the soreness she felt on the left side of her chest made her doubly leery.

At times, she felt like there may be a mass, but she'd pressed and prodded so much she'd convinced herself she'd caused the swelling and soreness.

Her legs shook as she sat on the paper-covered exam table. They shook because she was cold. That was all. She'd forgotten socks in her anxiety about coming. She didn't have any other reason for her legs to shake.

Dr. Coe walked into the room, a big smile covering her face. She gave Callie a quick hug. "How have you been? It's so good to see you." She motioned around the room. "Course, I know you'd rather we run into each other at the grocery store or the mall, but I'm still glad to see you." She tapped Callie's knee. "You look great. So, how are you?"

Callie's nerves calmed, and she knew seeing her mom's doctor had been the right choice. Dr. Coe had been a constant encouragement to her and her mother. The woman had tried every avenue to save Callie's mom. She'd even attended the funeral, hugged Callie and cried with her.

She told Dr. Coe about finishing nursing school and caring for her dad and hospice patients. For the first time, she experienced a peace relaying the story anew to someone. She lifted her hand. "I'm also getting married this October."

Dr. Coe narrowed her gaze. "That one boy. What was his name?" She snapped her fingers. "Kirk, right?"

Callie nodded. "Five years apart, but now we're back together."

"Sometimes time is what's needed." She pressed the

intercom and called for the nurse to join them in the room. "Okay, lie back and let's get this over with."

As she expected, Dr. Coe started with the breast examination. Callie lifted her left arm and tried not to groan when Dr. Coe felt the side of her chest. The doctor didn't say anything once she'd finished, but continued with the rest of the examination. Relief filled Callie. Maybe she'd been worried for nothing. It had been a few weeks since she'd bumped into the door, but if Dr. Coe didn't feel anything, everything must be all right. Dr. Coe tapped Callie's leg. "All done."

She sat up, and Dr. Coe pulled off her gloves, threw them in the trash then washed her hands. She turned around, and Callie's heart plunged at Dr. Coe's pursed lips. She remembered that expression. The blood rushed to Callie's ears as her heart beat against her chest.

Dr. Coe released a sigh. "You have a lump in your left breast."

Tears welled in Callie's eyes as she nodded. Fear filled her gut, and bile rose in her throat.

"Let's not be worried yet." She patted Callie's arm. "However, with your family history, we will be cautious. I want to do a needle biopsy right now."

"Now?" Callie's voice squeaked, and she cleared her throat, willing away the nausea that threatened to overcome her.

"Now. And I'll have the nurse set you up an appointment for a mammogram. Okay?"

Callie swiped her eyes with the back of her hand. What other option did she have? "Okay."

Dr. Coe's expression softened. "Listen. You're twenty-five years old. Chances are it is nothing. Just a bunch of bills for your insurance." She chuckled, and Callie couldn't help but grin. "But let's be sure."

Callie nodded.

Dr. Coe tapped her leg one last time. "Go ahead and put your bottoms on, but keep the robe up top. I'll go get everything ready and be right back."

Anxiety seized Callie's body when Dr. Coe left the room. Her hands started to shake, and she clasped them together. When that didn't work, she rubbed them on her already trembling legs. The room was so cold, which didn't help.

She tried to keep her mind blank. To not think. But images of her mother attacked her one after the other. Vomiting after a chemo treatment, not being able to eat, shaving her head when her hair started falling out. The weakness. Her mother, a woman who'd once been able to take on the world, or at least so it seemed to Callie, became a frail shell of a person.

Panic started in the base of Callie's gut. Her heart pounded, and her breath came out in shallow spurts. *Stay calm,* her mind whispered to her body.

The door opened and the nurse walked inside. She was a different woman than the one who'd helped Callie's mom. "I set up the mammogram for tomorrow afternoon. Does that work for you?"

Tomorrow afternoon? Dr. Coe was working fast. She must have a bad feeling about the lump. Callie hadn't felt as if it was a lump, but more like a swelling from hitting the door.

Sudden relief washed over her. She hadn't told Dr. Coe she'd run into the door. If the doctor knew that, she might not feel the urgency with the tests. But the mammogram wouldn't hurt, so Callie forced a smile at the nurse. "That should be fine."

The woman gave Callie the instructions. She could have repeated them verbatim to the lady, but she didn't say anything, simply listened. She took the orders and put them in her purse.

The woman left and several minutes passed before Dr. Coe and the nurse returned with the instruments needed for the biopsy.

Callie straightened her shoulders. "Dr. Coe, I forgot to tell you a couple of weeks ago I ran into the side of my screen door and whammed the left side of my body. I had a bruise on the left side of my breast for a while. It may still be swollen inside. That might be all you feel."

Callie knew she rambled, because even though she felt relief sharing the information with the doctor, anxiety still swirled within her.

Dr. Coe smiled, but it wasn't an expression of relief or that Callie's fall was a possibility for the lump. She pursed her lips, and Callie wanted to throw something at the older woman. "Let's hope that's all it is. Here we go."

Callie sucked in her breath and gripped the sides of the bed while Dr. Coe performed the biopsy. "All done."

Callie blinked back tears. That hurt. A lot.

"I'll call you as soon as I get the results. You'll be a little tender, but that's to be expected." She turned toward the nurse. "Mammogram tomorrow?"

"Yep. Can't wait."

Dr. Coe tucked the clipboard against her chest. "Your mom was such a fighter. If we'd caught it earlier, I know she'd have made it. You're young, and I can tell you've got that same spirit, and..." She paused then tapped Callie's leg for what seemed the hundredth time. "Again, let's not go down that road just yet. Chances are it is nothing."

The doctor and nurse walked out of the room, and Callie put on her shirt. *Chances are it is nothing* repeated over and over in her mind. Weren't those the same words she'd said to herself when she hit the door in the first place? Now, here she stood in the doctor's office, her left breast stinging worse than if she'd been bitten by a yellow jacket, making plans for a mammogram the next day.

She and Tammie planned to pick out flowers for the wedding the next day. Resolve settled upon her as she lifted her chin and peered up at the ceiling. They'd simply have to visit the florist in the morning. She had no intention of telling Kirk or anyone about the biopsy and mammogram. Not until she knew the results.

Her family background and her profession often led her to believe the worst, but the worst wasn't usually the case. If she stepped away from the situation and thought solely as a professional she would note that she was young and healthy and had recently injured the area. There was no reason to start traipsing down a path of morbid thinking.

Hefting her purse on her right shoulder, she walked out of the office. She stepped into the empty elevator and pushed the button. Looking up at her reflection, she said, "Remember, God is good. He's my refuge in trouble. He cares for me."

Chapter 15

Callie sat beside Tammie and flipped through the book of bouquets the floral shop had designed for past weddings. The room smelled heavenly with the warring of an array of blooms. Flowers never failed to lift Callie's spirits, each one beautiful in its own way. As the Bible said, God had adorned the fields with the flowers' splendor at no cost to the fields. *Course these flowers might just cost a penny or two.*

"Roses are a must," said Tammie as she pointed to a bouquet of yellow, red, salmon and burnt-orange blooms. Callie furrowed her brow. She'd never seen burnt-orange roses, and she wondered how they got them to look like that, because they didn't look sprayed.

Tammie flipped the page, and Callie pressed her finger against the photo of a simple arrangement of twelve white roses. The picture showed a long red ribbon at the base of the bouquet. "This is perfect for my flowers, only with a green ribbon instead of red." She waved her hand. "Or maybe no color at all. Simply white flowers and a white ribbon."

"I agree. It's simple but elegant." Tammie pointed to a picture on the following page. "What about this arrangement for Pamela?"

Callie looked at the arrangement of yellow-and-red roses, orange carnations and white daisies. The rustic brown ribbon seemed to enhance the colors of the flowers. It reminded her of a hike through the woods on a warm autumn day. Her primary color for the wedding was green, but the arrangement would be a terrific complement to Pamela's dress. Callie nodded. "I wouldn't change it at all."

The bell on the front door dinged, and Callie saw Pamela walk in. Her soon-to-be sister-in-law smiled with genuine pleasure. Callie marveled at the sight. Pamela had acted mopey and weighted down the past several weeks. Callie knew Tammie and Mike worried. She'd been concerned, as well.

Tammie motioned Pamela to them. She held up the book and showed her the bouquet. "What do you think?"

"I love it. Guess what?"

"What?" Callie and Tammie responded in unison.

Pamela lifted her fist and pumped the air. "Got an A on my first paper."

"Woohoo!" Tammie whooped. "I knew you could do it."

Pamela pursed her lip. "I wasn't so sure. You know it's been a while." She made a fist. "But I researched what needed to be done. Told myself that I could do this. It took some determination and some hard work. I'd done well in school when I wanted to, and I knew

I had the brains to get the job done. Just had to pump myself up a bit."

Tammie cheered. "I knew God would help you through it."

Callie frowned as Pamela's expression hardened. She turned away and touched a bouquet of yellow flowers on the table beside her. "These are pretty."

Distracted, Tammie hopped up and touched the bouquet. "They are lovely. We'll have to incorporate them in some way. Maybe for the reception." She clapped her hands then touched Callie's shoulder. "Mike and Kirk almost have the barn all cleaned out. It won't be the fanciest reception ever, but we'll still make it look great."

"You're already doing too much. We don't even need a reception."

Tammie lifted her hand. "We'll have none of that kind of discussion."

She made her way to the other side of the shop to find the florist, and Callie bent down and sniffed the inviting scent. She didn't know the kind, but she agreed she wanted them in the wedding. She straightened and studied Pamela. "I'm glad you're enjoying school."

"It's great. Giving me a sense of individuality. I'm not solely working on my parents' farm and raising kids, but I'm doing something for myself, as well."

Callie chewed the inside of her cheek. Pamela's sentiments weren't wrong exactly, but her tone and demeanor when she said them made Callie uncomfortable. She sounded angry and cold, and trepidation swelled in Callie's gut. "Have you heard from Jack lately?"

Pamela narrowed her gaze. "How did you know about that?"

Callie tried to recollect the origin of the knowledge.

Hadn't Pamela told her? She cringed. No. It was Kirk, and he'd asked her not to say anything. "Well, I…"

"Kirk has a big mouth." She placed her hand on her hip. "But so you know, no, I have not heard from Jack since Kirk told him to leave me alone." She smacked her pant leg. "And good riddance to him. The girls and I don't need a man, anyway."

Callie cringed. The bitterness showed itself full force, and she knew Pamela would take up a larger part of her prayer time. "I'm sorry…"

Pamela lifted her hand. "It's fine." Her expression softened. "Tell Kirk not to worry. His little sister is okay." She shrugged. "In fact, I've never been better."

Callie knew better. Pamela had built a wall. Callie watched as she walked to Tammie and started talking flowers with her and the florist. If anyone recognized construction in a gal's heart meant to protect her from pain, it was Callie. And Pamela had been working with some inner tools, and a wall had been formed.

Empathy filled Callie. She knew how Pamela felt. Frustrated. Tired. Burdened. She also knew Pamela couldn't fix the problems. Only God could mend her heart.

Callie glanced at the clock on the wall above a swag of purple flowers and ribbons. She'd need to hurry up this appointment. The mammogram was in a little over an hour.

And what am I going to do if I get bad news? Am I going to simply sit at Jesus's feet, believing that all will be well and that He'll heal me?

She swallowed the knot that formed in her throat.

Like He healed Momma?

She hefted her purse higher on her right shoulder and

closed her eyes. She would not go there. No dwelling on negative thoughts. Everything within her believed this was only a test to see if she would be faithful to God or if she would run when times got tough. A test, that was all. Not cancer. Not bad news.

She opened her eyes then walked to the other side of the shop to join Tammie, Pamela and the florist. She tapped her cell phone. "We'll have to hurry. I have an appointment in an hour."

Tammie furrowed her brows. "What for?"

"Doctor's appointment."

Tammie cocked her head. "I thought you went to the doctor yesterday. Is everything all right?"

"It's fine. Just a checkup."

Pamela released an exaggerated sigh. "I hate those."

The florist leaned close to Callie and Pamela and whispered, "Me, too."

Tammie frowned. "But I know you said you went..."

Callie touched Tammie's arm. "It's nothing. Just a checkup, like I said."

And that was what is would be. An uncomfortable X-ray proving no abnormal cells in her body. God was good. He was her refuge. He cared for her. She'd quoted the scripture a bunch of times in a ton of ways. God had given her the verse. She knew He wanted her to believe Him. Everything would be fine.

Jacobs Family Farm closed to the regular public on Labor Day so the family could enjoy time together. Originally, the plan had been just a cozy affair of his parents, Pamela and the girls, Ben, Callie and him. Somehow a couple of gals in Pamela's English class received word of the gathering, and they decided to come. As did a few families from the church. A couple of neighbors, including the middle-schooler Justin's family. His nieces invited a few friends, and Ben brought three guys home with him from the university. What started out to be a quaint gathering for immediate family soon included more than fifty people.

Not that Kirk minded. For the most part he sat back, played a little corn hole and tossed horseshoes. He and Dad were in charge of the grilling, but it didn't take too much effort to throw burgers and hot dogs on a grill, wait a few minutes and then flip them over.

The women, on the other hand, hustled back and forth, inside and outside the house, refilling various foods and taking emptying dishes inside. And he wouldn't have minded that so much if it didn't take away from him being able to spend time with Callie. But she was one of the gals running back and forth.

She'd seemed anxious the past few days, kind of snapped at him when he talked to her. His dad assured him wedding jitters had gotten the best of her, and Kirk hoped his dad was right. Still, his gut told him something else was going on. She walked out the back door and greeted a neighbor with a ready smile. He brushed the concern away. Her nerves probably had gotten the best of her. They reunited, fell in love and planned to marry all in six months' time. *And I'd tie the knot today if I could.*

He spied Pamela on the deck talking with her friends from college. She laughed several times, seeming happy to be around them. It warmed his heart to see her with them. She'd been forlorn, but the past few weeks she'd come out of her shell again. At times, she snapped a bit too quickly and came off gruffer than he'd ever known her, but her confidence had grown, and that was a good thing. Wasn't it?

A hand bore down on his shoulder. "Come on, big brother, let's play corn hole."

Kirk stood. "All right."

They walked to the corn hole game, and Kirk bent down and picked up the orange bags. Ben pointed to his friends then back at him and Kirk. "Spence and Alan against me and Kirk."

Alan scooped up the white bags. "Hmm…did you pick Kirk 'cause he's some kind of professional corn bag thrower?"

Kirk tossed a bag and caught it. "I'm not too bad."

Spence grabbed two bags from Alan and started juggling. "I'm not too bad, either."

Ben clasped his hand and rubbed them together. "All right. Sounds like we got us a good game."

Kirk stepped beside the board. "I'm going to need a couple of practice shots."

"Sounds good." Ben took two bags from Kirk. "We each get two practice throws."

Kirk lined up his throw. The object was to toss the corn-filled bag into the hole for three points, or at least toss it on to the board for one point. He turned to his brother. "Playing to fifteen? I'm going to have to grill before long."

Ben shrugged. "That's fine."

Kirk tossed his practice shots and swished both through the hole. He pumped his fist, and Ben high-fived him. He still had it. Ben tossed and hit the board the first time and then landed the second through the hole. Not bad. Alan missed the board altogether on both tosses, but Spence nailed the hole both times. If Alan could manage to hit the board, this would be a good game.

Kirk and Spence stood beside each other. Kirk tossed the orange bag first and hit the board. Spence tossed and swished through the hole.

Ben growled. "Come on, Kirk. Where's that perfect shot?"

Kirk laughed, knowing his brother had to be kidding, but when he missed again, and Spence's landed through the hole a second time, he watched as Ben's face turned red. He extended his hands, palms up. "Ben, it's just a game."

"You can play better than that and you know it."

Kirk frowned. When had Ben become so competitive? He remembered the Fourth of July celebration, and Ben's determination to win some silly stuffed animal. He'd never seen his brother act that way. The same way he acted today.

In a matter of minutes, Spence and Alan had beaten them. Kirk placed the bags on the board. "That was fun, but Dad looks like he needs a break."

Ben's face blazed with frustration. "Dad is fine. We're playing again. Best two out of three."

Kirk started to protest, but his dad lifted the spatula in the air. "I'm fine. Play another game with them, Kirk. You'd be a better partner than me."

"I don't know about that."

Kirk frowned at his brother. The comment slithered under his breath, but it was rude and ridiculous and uncalled for. When playing a game, someone had to lose. Every time. Winning had its perks, but losing was part of playing.

He picked up the corn bags again. Part of him wanted

to not worry about his toss, just fling the silly thing and let it land where it landed. But that would be spiteful, which would be as bad as Ben being a poor loser.

After Spence tossed the first through the hole, Kirk followed with one of his own. Spence tossed another, and the next time Kirk hit the board. The game continued until Kirk missed a last shot through the hole and Alan and Spence beat them again. Kirk shook Spence's hand. "Great job, man. You're a gifted corn hole player."

Spence blew on his knuckles and rubbed them on his shirt. "Well, I try."

Ben stomped to them. "I can't believe you missed again."

Kirk glared at his brother. "What is the matter with you?"

Ben threw up his hands. "Were you throwing the game on purpose or what?"

Kirk bit his lip and counted to ten to keep from giving Ben a tongue-lashing they'd both regret. By the time his temper had settled Ben stomped off with Alan alongside him. Kirk turned to Spence. "Does he always act like that?"

Spence scrunched his nose. "If he loses. Dude, your brother's intense." He shrugged. "Course, he usually doesn't lose."

Kirk watched as Spence walked away and caught up with Ben and Alan. Shaking his head, he took the spatula from his dad and grilled the meat as his mother brought it out to him.

Callie brought him a plate of hot dogs. Leaning down, he planted a quick kiss on her lips. She swatted his arm. "Not in front of everyone."

He laughed and turned back to the grill then jumped

at the figure standing beside him. "You scared the life out of me." Recognizing the person, he put down the spatula and gave the guy a quick hug. "Zack. I didn't know you were coming. How you doing?"

Zack shrugged, but Kirk noted his coloring had improved since the last time he saw him. "I have good days and bad days."

Kirk picked up the spatula again and pointed it at Zack's arm. "Your cast is off."

"Yep. Over two weeks now."

"That's great."

"I finished the gazebo."

"You did?"

"Yeah. It's really nice. Greta would have liked it." He pointed to Heather. Kirk would have never recognized her. She'd cut her hair and must have had on makeup because her face looked different. "Heather helped. She was my second hand when I couldn't use it."

Kirk nodded. "I'm glad."

"Listen, I'm happy for you and Callie. You two always seemed perfect for each other." His lower lip quivered. "But I don't think I'll be at the wedding."

"Not a problem at all."

Kirk had to keep from chuckling aloud when Zack turned and sat beside Heather. No one was invited to the wedding. Only the same people who had originally been asked to the cookout. But somehow everyone ended up saying they were coming. The wedding was in just over a month, and they'd sent no invitations. And didn't plan to. If people showed up, they showed up. The only person he cared about seeing there was Callie.

Chapter 16

Kirk lifted his shoulders then pushed them back then pushed them forward then pushed them back again. "Too tight."

The woman standing in front of him pursed her lips. Her features squished together making her look as if she'd sucked on a lemon, and her hair had been tied up so tight on the top of her head that her eyes slanted. "Mr. Jacobs, this is the seventh tuxedo jacket you've tried on. I assure you it fits."

Kirk growled when his dad busted out laughing. "Now son, are you going with a bow or a tie? What about a vest?"

Horror raced through Kirk's mind, and he gaped at the exasperated woman. "Surely I don't have to pick all that out."

The woman shook her head. "No, you do not. Callie and your mother came in more than two weeks ago with instructions on what to order." She pursed her lips again before she added, "Of course, they said you'd be in the next day."

Ben huffed. "It took this long to get him to come down here. If I didn't know better I'd think he sleeps in his boots and oversize belt buckle." He lifted Kirk's favorite buckle off the back of the chair. "I mean, seriously man, how long have you had this thing?"

Kirk tried to remember when Mom bought it for him. Christmas. He knew that. It had been a long time. Finally, he shrugged. "High school, maybe." He pointed to the design. "But look at it. Doesn't it remind you of the farm with the cows in the front and the barn and silo in the back?"

Ben blew out a breath. "Big brother, you'd be lucky for any woman to have you. God must be looking down with favor on you."

"Amen to that," the lady who'd helped fit him mumbled.

He scowled at her, and she looked down and started arranging ties on the table beside her. He didn't much like that woman. There wasn't a thing wrong with a man who didn't want to be all squeezed up in some monkey suit.

His dad lifted up a vest and tie. "Would you like to try on the rest of your attire?"

Kirk growled. "Seriously?"

Dad nodded. "You'd better. You only have to wear it one evening of one day, then you'll have Callie for the rest of your life."

Kirk grabbed the clothes out of his dad's hands. If they'd put it like that to begin with he'd have been able to endure all the putting on and taking off.

After being fitted in a getup that he swore still felt too tight, he tore out of the monkey suit and put on his worn jeans and plaid button-down shirt. He grinned at his reflection as he buckled his oversize buckle then slipped into his molded-to-his-feet boots. For the first time in over an hour he felt like himself again.

His dad and Ben decided to get a bite to eat, but Kirk declined. He grabbed a burger then headed back to the farm. Feeling a few jitters of his own, he grabbed his fishing pole and cooler of bait out of the barn and trekked back to the pond.

He didn't care if he caught any fish. Putting on that monkey suit made him feel all stuffy and stuck. He wanted to marry Callie. No concerns or quandaries about that. But being married would change things.

For years, he'd lived pretty much for himself. If he wanted to eat, he ate. If farm work was done and he wanted a nap, he napped. If he wanted some time away from the family, he didn't go to the main house. In a little over a month, all that would change.

Callie would be his priority, and he wanted that. He longed to come home in the evenings and find her there. To turn over in bed in the morning and see her beautiful face.

But that didn't mean there wouldn't be an adjustment.

Reaching the pond, he pulled a mealworm out of the cooler, shut the lid and sat down on top of it. He baited his pole then flung the line into the water.

Callie'd been acting a little funny. Jitters, his dad had told him several times. He hoped so. He'd never seen anyone with wedding jitters, except maybe what he felt was what she felt, as well.

And when he thought about his siblings. Well, he had no idea what was going on with the two of them. Pamela started school and all of the sudden she was the educated professor who thought she knew better than all of them. And Ben. Kirk shook his head. Where had his competitive craziness come from?

He felt a tug on the line so he stood and reeled in his catch. Grabbing the good-size bluegill, he pulled the hook out of its mouth then tossed the fish back into the water. He baited the hook and flung it back in the pond again.

I've got a lot on my mind right now, God. I'm excited about the wedding. A little nervous, too. But I'm glad to have Callie. Nerves or no nerves, I love you. But Pamela...

His line jerked again. He reeled in another bluegill, yanked out the hook and tossed the little critter back into the pond.

He sat back down on the cooler. *I don't know what's going on with Pamela. I don't even know how to pray...*

The line bobbed again. Standing back up, he reeled in the line. This time a bass hung from the hook. He chortled as he pulled out the hook and tossed the fish back in the pond.

He gazed up at the clear blue sky. "I suppose I'm doing a little too much thinking today. Must be all I need to do is enjoy this fine weather you've given us and spend a little time catching fish."

Baiting the hook again, he flung it back into the water. From now on, he was keeping the fish he caught. The weatherman predicted a sunny sky for the following day, which meant it would be good weather for a fish fry. And the way things were going, he'd be able to feed the whole family, and probably anyone else who decided to show up.

Callie cut the extra edge from the photo of her and Kirk when she was a freshman and he was a sophomore. The youth group had a fall party, and they were snuggled up on hay bales piled up in a trailer. He'd given her their first kiss on that hay ride.

She picked up another picture of the two of them beside a Christmas tree. If memory served her right, it was her junior year. She spotted her mother's necklace around her neck, and she crinkled her nose. Definitely junior year. Her mother, fearing the cancer would eventually win her fight for her life, had given Callie the keepsake that Christmas.

Another picture showed the two of them on the front porch sitting on the swing and holding hands. There was one of her with Ben, Pamela and Kirk. She looked at Tammie. "I can't believe you still have all these."

Tammie huffed. "Why wouldn't I? You were like one of my own children." She lifted up a photo of Kirk and Callie in the front seat and Pamela and Jack in the backseat of her old car. "Jack, too."

Callie slid the photograph she'd cropped into the leaf-trimmed frame Tammie had purchased for the wedding. She motioned toward the thirty or more matching frames. "Do we have enough pictures for all of these?"

"Why, of course."

"And what in the world will you do with all these frames after the wedding? Surely, you don't want thirty leaf-covered frames sitting around the B and B."

Tammie furrowed her brows. "Pamela's crafty. I'm

sure she'll think of something we can make so we can sell them."

Callie spied a picture of her and Kirk on her sixteenth birthday. He'd bought her a dozen red roses and a matchbox car, promising he'd buy her a real one in a few years' time. She showed Tammie the picture. "I'll have to tell him I'm still waiting on that car."

"Oh, there will be plenty of cars. Once the grandkids come into play, there will be minivans." Tammie pressed her hands against her chest. "I'm looking forward to the minivans."

Callie giggled at her soon-to-be mother-in-law's dramatics as she fit another picture into a frame. "These pictures will be a lot of fun at the reception."

"Especially since it will be more than just a family affair."

Callie rolled her eyes. "I know. It's almost gotten out of hand. What number are we up to?"

"My last count was seventy-five." Tammie snapped her fingers. "I just remembered I put a box of Kirk's graduation photos in the attic. I know there will be tons of the two of you in it. I'll be right back."

Callie stood with Tammie and walked to the front door. "You want me to help?"

"No, no. It will only take a minute."

A black sedan pulled into the driveway, drove past the main house and stopped behind Callie's car.

"Looks like you have company. I'll be right back."

Recognizing the driver, Callie didn't respond to Tammie. Fear filled her heart as Dr. Coe got out of the car. *Please be a congratulations-on-your-wedding house call.*

The older woman's somber expression heaped dread

onto Callie's fear. Without a greeting, she opened the screen door and Dr. Coe stepped inside. She clasped her hands as she gazed around the cabin's living room. "You have such a sweet home, Callie."

"What is it?"

Callie knew she'd been abrupt, but she didn't want to make small talk. The last time she'd seen Dr. Coe in her home was the day she'd buried her mother.

"You're right to assume I had a reason for coming." She motioned toward the couch. "May we sit?"

Callie moved several photos off the cushion and placed them on the coffee table. She settled into the padded rocking chair across from the couch.

Dr. Coe pointed to the pictures. "These look lovely. Photos of you and your fiancé, I presume."

Callie rubbed her now clammy hands together. "Please, Dr. Coe."

"Yes, well, I wanted to tell you in person. I was so fond of your mother. I've never really been a praying woman, but I was intrigued by her faith, even in the midst of so many setbacks."

Callie scratched the side of her head. The doctor needed to spit it out.

"The biopsy was positive for cancer cells, Callie, and there is a small mass on your left breast."

Callie leaned back in the chair, sucked in a deep breath and pressed her lips together. She'd quoted the scripture from Nahum repeatedly, claiming it to mean the test would come back negative. But deep in her spirit, she'd known. Even from the day she'd run into the door. She released the breath and looked at Dr. Coe. "So, what's the plan?"

She handed her a packet of papers. "I made your

appointment with the oncologist for this week. Based on the mammogram, my guess is he will schedule a lumpectomy as soon as possible. With your mother having had breast cancer, I assume they will want to do chemotherapy and radiation, or at the very least, just radiation."

Callie nodded. She already knew the drill. It hadn't been necessary to ask. It was simply the first thing that popped out of her mouth. She stood and extended her hand to the doctor. "Okay. Thanks for coming. I appreciate you driving out to tell me yourself."

Dr. Coe stood and wrapped both hands around Callie's. "Listen, you are young. The mass is very small on the mammogram. Your situation is not the same as your mother's." She pointed to the pictures on the table. "I know this boy's family. If he's half as good as his parents, he'll stand by you through it all. Are you listening to me?"

"Yes." *No. I'm not listening at all. You have no idea what this is like. You watch cancer. You treat cancer. You haven't lived cancer.*

Dr. Coe gave her a hug, and Callie used all her effort to squeeze back. Remaining stoic and calm, she said again, "I really appreciate you telling me in person."

And she did appreciate it. Dr. Coe had proven to be a very nice woman. She held the front door as the doctor walked out. She watched as she got in her car, waved and then drove away.

God, I thought we were starting fresh. Haven't I had enough pain in my life? Both parents? Wasn't that enough?

Her father's frustrated, embarrassed expression when he left her and her mother filtered through her mind.

She remembered her mother's sunken eyes and cheeks the last weeks of her life. She wouldn't do that to Kirk. Make him regret being married to her. Make him watch her die.

She raced into the bedroom and yanked the suitcase out from under the bed. Moving as fast as her hands would allow, she shoved as many clothes as she could grab into the suitcase and zipped it shut. Rushing into the bathroom, she scooped all of her beauty products in one sweep into a duffel bag.

Tammie had already been gone longer than Callie would have expected. Trying to hurry, she threw shoes into another bag. In two trips, she'd packed all she could in the backseat of the car.

With one last look back at Kirk's house, she swiped away the single tear that escaped her eye. She had wanted to be Mrs. Kirk Jacobs so badly. But it wasn't meant to be.

Callie was already in the car and halfway down the driveway when she saw Tammie walk out the back door of the main house, holding a small box in her hand. Her brows were furrowed in confusion as she waved for Callie to come back.

Pain laced through her heart as she shifted her gaze away from the woman and the house and onto the main road. She turned left. She'd have to go back to the only place she knew to go. Her old boss had promised her a job any time she decided to return. She wouldn't be able to tell him the cancer prognosis she'd received, but Callie figured she'd be able to be evasive for a while. It had taken several months before her mother became too ill.

She thought of her father leaving everything in his will to his brother and nephew. Bitterness welled inside her. Now would have been a good time for her to have some provision from him. He'd left her and her mom. Despite that, when he needed help, she'd dropped everything and gone to his aid. *I need him now, and he's ditched me again.* She smacked the top of the steering wheel. *Even from the grave he left me to fend for myself.*

On impulse, she touched her mother's charm around her neck. She'd draw strength from her memory, from the many good times they'd had together. Where else would she be able to find strength?

Chapter 17

Kirk frowned when he saw his mother hurrying toward him, waving papers in her hand. He turned off the tractor and hopped off the seat. She didn't have any business scurrying around the fields like that. She'd be sore all evening, or worse reinjure her ankle. Stopping just in front of him, she placed her hand on her chest and panted.

He put his hand on her shoulder. "Mom, what is it? Nothing could be so important that you come running out here—"

"She's gone." His mother swallowed then tilted her head back and sucked in another breath.

"What? Who's gone?"

She shoved the papers in his hands. "Callie. She must have forgotten these."

Kirk shook his head. She wasn't gone. She couldn't be. They were getting married in a month's time. She'd probably just had to run an errand or something. And what were these papers his mom was waving in his face?

He grabbed the stack from her. Callie's name was printed at the top. Stapled beside it was a business card with an appointment date and time written on it. He read the name of the doctor and then the man's title. Oncologist.

His heart sank, and his stomach knotted. "Mom, what is this?"

"We were at the cabin, putting pictures in frames for the reception. Having a great time sifting through old memories." She covered her mouth with the tips of her fingers and shook her head. "I remembered I had another box of photos, and I ran back to the house. I knew I recognized the woman that pulled up. I just couldn't place her."

Kirk scratched his forehead. "Mom, what are you talking about?" He pointed to the papers. "What does that have to do with this?"

"Don't you see? The woman was her mom's doctor, the one who found the cancer." She rubbed her hands along the sides of her thighs. "I knew something was wrong the other day at the flower shop. I knew she'd gone to the doctor once. There was no reason for her to have to go again. I should have pressed her for more information." She looked up at him, her eyes brimming with tears. "She said everything was fine, and I didn't want to believe otherwise."

He wrapped his arm around his mother's shoulder. An oncologist meant cancer. The knots in his stomach tightened, and his legs felt weak as he tried to keep his mind from going to the worst of possibilities. "It's okay.

I'll talk to her when she gets back. She probably just needs to blow off some steam—"

"No." His mom pushed away from him. "You don't understand. Her clothes are gone. She left."

Kirk growled as he dropped the tractor key in her hand. "Drive the tractor back. It's too far for you to walk."

Without waiting for her to respond, he ran to the cabin. Sweat trailed down his face, and his chest burned once he reached it. Throwing open the front door, he halted at the disarray. That ugly picture with the horse was gone, as were several other knickknacks she'd kept around the room. He walked to the bedroom. As his mom said, the drawers had been pulled out and emptied, just like the closet and the bathroom.

He sat on the edge of the bed, leaned forward, placing his elbows on his legs and pressing his head against his hands. Where would she have gone?

God, why did she run? She had to know I would be with her through it all, help her as she fought whatever lay ahead.

He thought of her dad leaving when her mother's cancer reached its worst. Callie endured the last year, watching her mother fight and lose. Knowing Callie, she didn't want him to see her so sick.

He sat up and wrapped his arms around his waist. "God, I don't want to see her so sick. Why, Lord?"

His thoughts shifted to the Fourth of July. Greta had passed away only a week before and he and Callie talked about God's sovereignty, even when they couldn't see His plan. She'd told him she loved him, that she was willing to endure pain with the love.

Resolve settled into his core. He stood. "God, I let her leave once. I won't let her do it again."

He walked into the kitchen and rummaged through papers on the countertop. Surely, there would be some clue about where she would go. He didn't believe she'd go to her uncle's or cousin's house. The only people she talked about from those five years away were her patients, and to his knowledge, they had all passed on.

He snapped his fingers. That was it. She'd have gone back to the hospice job. She'd told him on several occasions how much love she'd had for her patients, and that her boss said he'd hire her back in a minute. It was the only thing that made sense.

Rushing out of the cabin, he ran to his house, grabbed the truck keys and headed down the road. He stopped at a four-way stop sign. He didn't feel right. Something was missing.

Realization pressed on his heart, and he turned the truck to the right. After a few miles of pleading with God to show him the words to say, he pulled into the town's cemetery. Following the winding road toward the back, his heart lifted when he saw her car.

He parked behind her then hopped out of the cab. Pressing the cool keys to his lips, he muttered, "Show me, Lord. Give me the right words."

Stepping onto the graveled path that led to her mother's gravesite, his mind traveled back to the day of her burial. He'd held Callie close as she cried, her head resting on his shoulder. Then and there, he'd decided to be there for her for the rest of her life.

Then I panicked, broke it off and let her leave.

He picked up the pace, knowing she'd be a little ways beyond the next tree.

But times have changed. I've grown up. I'm here, and she's not getting rid of me so easily.

Shoving his hands in his pockets, he chewed his bottom lip when he saw her. She sat on her knees, hands pressed against the top of her legs. She didn't seem to be crying, just staring at the headstone.

Walking up behind her, he placed one hand on her shoulder. She didn't flinch, and he knew she'd felt him walking up beside her.

"I forgot the papers Dr. Coe gave me at the cabin."

Her voice sounded just above a whisper, and he nodded even though she wasn't looking at him. "Yep."

She still didn't look back, and he waited, begging God to show him what to say.

"I guess you read them."

"I did."

"You know what kind of doctor an oncologist is."

Her words didn't come out as a question. She knew better than to ask. Of course, he knew what kind of doctor she had to see the following week. "You know I do."

He knelt on the ground beside her and read her mother's name, birthday and date of death on the headstone. "*Beloved Mother*" was written at the bottom. And she had been beloved, not only by Callie, but all the people who knew her.

Swallowing the knot in his throat, he took Callie's hand in his. She turned toward him, and he rubbed the top of her hand with his thumb. "I let you go once. I refuse to let that happen again."

Callie stared into his deep eyes, honesty and love peering back at her. "I know. I panicked when I saw Dr. Coe get out of that car. I know what cancer looks like."

Kirk lifted his chin, determination gleamed in his eye, but she still detected the hint of fear. "We'll get through this."

She smiled. "You're right. One way or another, depending on how bad it is."

Kirk shook his head. "Don't talk like that. Everything will be fine. You're—"

She lifted her free hand and placed her finger on his lips. "Kirk, you have to be ready for that."

He pulled her hand down. Sincerity shone in his expression, and he lifted his chin, his telltale sign of an effort to keep his lip from quivering. "I'm gonna be honest. I'm scared."

Tears filled her eyes. She loved this man. "I am, too."

He pulled her into his arms, and for the first time since hearing the results of the test, she allowed herself to cry. Kirk's arms were strong, his chest broad and firm, giving her the physical comfort she needed.

God, I'm sorry I freaked out. I know You have a plan. A sob caught in the back of her throat. *But I want Your plan to include life here on earth with Kirk.* She felt a slow grin lifting her lips. *And as many kids as he wants.*

"I wanna say a prayer for you, for us."

Callie nodded, keeping her face pressed against his chest. She wrapped her arms around him as he spoke words of praise for God's love and faith in his sovereignty. She squeezed him tight when his voice shook as he petitioned God to heal her and use the cancer as a means to bring Him glory.

When he finished the prayer, Callie lifted her head off his chest and sat back on her knees. Kirk gripped her hand as if he feared she'd run away if he let go. "So, what's going to happen?"

She pursed her lips. "I'll find out for sure next week."

"*We'll* find out for sure."

Callie smiled. "My guess is they'll perform a lumpectomy."

He furrowed his brows.

She continued. "Surgery to remove the lump."

He nodded, and she noticed his bottom lip moving, and she knew he chewed the inside of his mouth something fierce. "And that's it? That's not so bad, right?"

She shrugged. "I may have to have chemo and radiation."

A shiver raced through her when she said the words aloud. The vomiting, nausea and weakness didn't scare her. Though it hurt her vanity a bit, she wasn't too upset about the knowledge that she'd probably lose her hair. She feared the look in his eyes when he saw her sickness and couldn't do anything to help. She couldn't count the times she'd prayed God would allow her to take her mother's discomfort, if only for a day.

"Whatever it takes. We'll do it together." He stood, holding her hand up until she stood with him. "But I do believe it's going to be okay, that you're going to be healed. Completely."

Callie didn't know how to respond. She'd seen too much death to say she believed all would end well. Thinking clinically, she knew the odds were probably good. Her age and the small size of the lump should offer her a good prognosis.

We're going to believe the best, but prepare for the worst. Her mom's words during the last few years of her life wafted through her mind. Callie had spent so much time dealing with the worst, she hadn't given a lot of thought to believing the best.

God, I'm going to believe the best first.

She kissed her fingertips then pressed them against the top of the headstone. Still holding Kirk's hand, she turned and they walked back to the car and truck.

He whispered in her ear. "I'm not letting you drive back to the cabin."

She crinkled her nose and gaped at him. "What?"

"There's no way I'm going to chance you trying to hightail it out of here again."

"I'm going back. I'd decided to go back to the farm the minute I parked the car."

"Doesn't matter. I'm not letting you go. Mom and Dad won't mind coming back for your car."

She stepped in front of him and put her hand on his chest. "Tell you what. I'll go with you if we drive my car and you help me unpack all my stuff. They can come back and get your truck."

Kirk groaned, and she had to bite back a laugh. She knew he didn't like for anyone else to drive his precious F150. With a low growl, he mumbled, "Fine, but I'm driving."

He opened the door for her, and she slipped inside. He got in the driver's seat, and she handed him the keys. Studying her for a moment, he said, "What about the wedding?"

"I don't know." She touched the tip of her hair. "I want to have my hair in our wedding pictures, and I'd say the surgery will be pretty quick."

A slow grin lifted his lips. "Then we'll move up the date."

"What?"

"You heard me. We're definitely not going to postpone it." He put the keys in the ignition. "We shouldn't have any trouble telling the place we'll need to switch dates."

"Well, seeing as the wedding is at the farm, I'd say you're right. The owners of our venue wouldn't mind at all."

Chapter 18

Callie sucked in a breath while Tammie tightened the bodice of the wedding dress.

"You doing okay?" asked Tammie.

Callie nodded. Almost two weeks had passed since the lumpectomy. She'd been diligent about wearing good support bras and completing the exercises the doctor prescribed. Her incision was healing nicely, and she'd had no complications.

They'd moved the wedding up a couple weeks, as the oncologist performed the lumpectomy the week she met with him. Since the doctor had gotten all the cancer with the first surgery, she'd start radiation treatments two days after the wedding.

Kirk promised they'd take a honeymoon once the treatments were complete and she felt up to it, but Callie didn't care. All she wanted was to enjoy being married to Kirk and hear her doctor say the cancer was in full remission.

"All done. Let me see you."

Tammie moved to the front of Callie. She cupped her mouth with her hands, and her eyes brimmed with tears. She reached for Callie's arm then pulled back. "Are you okay? Do I need to adjust anything?"

Callie shook her head. "I can't believe how good I feel." She lifted her hand. "Of course, I did just take a painkiller, and I am rather excited about the event. Later on, I may be whiny and weepy for your son, but right now, I feel pretty good."

Tammie touched a spiral curl that draped down Callie's cheek. "You whine and cry to that boy all you want. He won't mind a bit."

"So, may I see?"

Tammie harrumphed. "Of course, you can."

Tammie moved out of the way, and Callie stepped in front of the full-length mirror.

"Wow." The single word slipped through Callie's lips. The dress was perfect, and her hair and makeup were just as beautiful. Pamela spent well over an hour spiral curling small strands of hair, and then pinning them up in the back. Several spirals framed her face and neck.

"Your mother would be so proud."

Callie bit her bottom lip. She wished her mom could be here. Tammie would be a first-rate mother-in-law, but no one could take her mother's place. "I miss her so much."

"I know you do." Tammie touched her cheek. "I'd put my arms around you but I don't want to hurt you."

Callie laughed. "Thank you for being so good to me."

"I can't replace your mom, and I'd never try, but I love you like one of my own children."

Callie grabbed her hand and squeezed. "And I love you."

"It's about time to get started. Can I see her yet?"

Tammie opened the bedroom door to let Mike in. He let out a low whistle. "Aren't you the most beautiful bride ever?"

"Dad, that's what you said to me on my wedding day." Pamela walked in the door, holding the bouquet of white roses.

"Well, you were the most beautiful bride, too."

Pamela rolled her eyes. She handed Callie the flowers. "You look amazing."

"You don't look so bad yourself."

Pamela lifted one hand and twisted her hip. "Green does happen to be one of my best colors." She motioned for them to come out of the room. "The girls are already downstairs. It's time to get you all down there, as well."

Mike and Pamela walked out first. Callie took a few steps and Tammie lifted the train of the dress. It was too heavy for Callie to scoop up and hold. She felt pretty good, but she didn't want to take any chances trying to lift anything that heavy.

Once down the stairs, Tammie gave her a quick kiss on the cheek then hustled out the door. Ben was probably chompin' at the bit because he had to seat her before he could take his place beside Kirk.

Originally, they'd planned to have the wedding in front of the orchard and then clean out the barn for the reception. But Callie couldn't tolerate much walking. Instead, Kirk, Ben and his dad built an arch and placed it a little ways from the house. She and Mike would walk off the back porch and right onto the white runner covering the wedding aisle. They'd also set up a tent with tables and chairs a few feet away for the reception.

She hadn't been able to help decorate. Getting ready and participating in the wedding would make her sore enough. She hated that she couldn't help, though she knew Kirk and his family had done a terrific job. She couldn't wait to see it.

The music they'd chosen filled the air. Callie smiled at the lyrics that promised they'd love one another forever. The music changed, and she knew Pamela was walking down the aisle. After a few moments, she knew Emma and Emmy had to be walking down, dropping green, yellow, orange and red petals.

The beginning of "Wedding March" sounded, and Mike gently grabbed her elbow. "You ready?"

Callie's heart beat with excitement. Despite her gut reaction to run when Dr. Coe had shared the results of her tests, Callie felt complete peace. She longed to see the man who would soon be her husband. She smiled at Mike. "Absolutely ready."

He opened the door, and Callie gasped at the sight before her. Yellow, orange and red flowers hung from a white arch. Green bows wrapped around white chairs on both sides of the makeshift aisle.

And Kirk stood at the front. Gorgeous in his black tuxedo, he stared at her. His expression glowed with love for her, and Callie felt her heartbeat speed up again. In only a few steps, he would take her hands. She would gaze into his eyes and promise the rest of her life with him.

She took his breath away. He'd fallen for her sweet smile in high school. Years had passed, and now he loved every aspect of Callie—her faith, her determination, her compassion, and he still loved that sweet smile.

As she and his dad made their way toward him, he touched the ring buried in his front pocket. In a matter of moments, she would become his wife. He would promise to love and care for her the rest of their days. Wrapping his hand around the ring, he prayed, *Oh, God, may they be many.*

Once she reached him, he took her hands in his. Their minister talked of love and commitment, important reminders that he should listen to regarding marriage. And yet, the man's words sounded like jumbled murmurings. Kirk's senses only had room enough for his bride.

He drank in her beauty. The fancy curls framing her face. The gorgeous dress hugging her body. The expression of peace and love in her gaze.

He released her hand and cupped her cheek with his palm. She lifted her eyebrows in surprise then pressed her cheek against his hand. Such beautiful skin. So soft. For as many days as God allowed he would touch her, love her, care for her.

His turn came to say *I do*. He hadn't listened, but it didn't matter. Speaking the words, he knew the promise he made before God and his family and friends. He would honor his word in the good and bad. All the while, he would continue to pray for good. He'd enjoy every blissful moment and pocket them in his heart to help him through the rough days.

"By the power vested in me and the state of Tennessee—" their minister's voice broke his reverie "—I now pronounce you husband and wife."

Kirk didn't have to listen anymore. He knew what happened next. Stepping closer to Callie, he cupped her cheeks in his hands and pressed her lips to his. They were sweet, soft and smelled of peppermint. He longed to sweep her into his arms and carry her straight to the home he had shared with his brother. Their home now.

But he had to be careful not to hurt her. The time would come when he would wrap strong arms around her and hold her tight to himself. With everything in him, he believed healing would come.

Patience had never been his strongest point, but he would make it through. She kissed him again, and he relished the taste and feel of her lips against his. Opening his eyes, he saw the longing he felt reflected in her gaze. Contentment swelled within him. She'd come back to him. He'd continue to pray healing for her body, all the while praising God for a heart that was healed.

Epilogue

Two years later

Callie lifted the baby back ribs out of the oven. She looked at the clock and realized she needed to hurry a bit if she wanted to have dinner on the table before Kirk came in from working on the farm.

Her mind wandered to her scheduled doctor's visit earlier that day. Much like two years ago, she'd gone expecting a regular yearly visit. Once again, she'd received unexpected news.

Looking at the sonogram printout for what had to be the hundredth time, she traced the outlines with her finger. She believed nothing could top hearing the doctor say, "Congratulations. The cancer is in remission."

Until today.

She turned off the stove then poured the warmed baby peas into a serving dish. She did the same with the baby carrots and baby potatoes. After placing all the dishes on the kitchen table, she set out a plate and silverware for both of them. Sticking the printout inside their Bible, she placed it on the table beside Kirk's plate.

She glanced at the clock again. He was later than usual. Twirling the string to the hood of her sweatshirt, she pondered the many reactions Kirk might have. Her thoughts shifted to Pamela's frustration earlier that morning when she'd told Callie that Jack had contacted her wanting to see the girls. She knew what Kirk's reaction would be to that.

She shook her head, determined not to think of Jack or Pamela right now. This moment was about her and Kirk and…

The front door opened, and Callie bit her bottom lip. Everything in her wanted to run into the other room, throw her arms around her husband and tell him all she'd learned at the doctor's office today.

"Smells terrific in here!" he hollered from the front room.

"Thanks," she called back as she placed her hands on the corners of her lips, trying to force the cheesy grin from her face. "I made baby back ribs."

"Great, I'm starving." He walked into the kitchen and went straight to the sink to wash his hands.

Taking deep breaths to calm her beating heart, she sat at the table. He joined her, and she watched as he scooped up a large spoonful of each dish. He motioned toward the food. "You gonna eat?"

She blinked. "Yes. Of course." She lifted a spoonful of peas. "I love baby peas."

"Yeah. They're pretty good."

"And baby potatoes."

He nodded.

"And these baby carrots cooked up nicely."

He blew out a breath. "They look wonderful, but it's been a long day, and I'm starving."

He reached across the table and took her hands in his. While he offered the dinner prayer, she bit her bottom lip. She didn't know if she should fuss at him for being impatient or laugh that he wasn't getting it. Finished with the prayer, he took a big bite of ribs.

"So, how are the baby back ribs?" she asked.

He licked his fingers, then scooped up a forkful of peas. "Delicious."

She cocked her head. "What about the baby peas?"

"Good."

He shoveled several more bites into his mouth, and Callie blew out an exasperated sigh. He pointed his fork at her plate. "Why aren't you eating?"

Deciding to try a different approach, she folded her hands together and placed them in her lap. "I went to see Dr. Coe today."

His face blanched. "I thought that was tomorrow. What did she say?"

Guilt niggled at her at the fear that wrapped his features. She waved her hands in front of her. "Nothing bad." She nodded toward the Bible. "See that paper sticking out. If you'll look at it, you'll see they did find a little something."

Pulling out the sonogram printout, he furrowed his brows and wrinkled his nose. "What in the world?"

Understanding wrapped his features as he lifted his brows then took in the dishes on the table. He pointed to the carrots. "Baby carrots?"

She grinned.

"And baby peas?"

She covered her mouth with her fingertips and nodded as tears filled her eyes.

He stood, almost knocking over his chair, and raced around the table. Wrapping his arms around her, he said, "Baby back ribs? Is there a reason for all this food?"

She giggled. "Yes."

"Oh, Cals." He planted kisses on her forehead, her eyes, her nose and then her lips. Releasing her, he pointed to the white peanut shapes on the sonogram. "Which one is our baby?"

She giggled again. "Both of them."

* * * * *

SPECIAL EXCERPT FROM

Love Inspired

Jolie Sheridan gets more than she bargained for when she arrives at Sunrise Ranch for a teaching job.

Read on for a preview of
HER UNFORGETTABLE COWBOY by Debra Clopton.

Jolie followed Morgan outside. There was a large gnarled oak tree still bent over as it had been all those years ago. She didn't stop until she reached it, turning his way only after they were beneath the wide expanse of limbs.

Morgan crossed his arms and studied the tree. "I remember having to climb up this tree and talk you down after you scrambled up to the top and froze."

She hadn't expected him to bring up old memories—it caught her a little off guard. "I remember how mad you were at having to rescue the silly little new girl."

A hint of a smile teased his lips, fraying Jolie's nerves t the edges. It had been a long time since she'd seen that mile.

"I got used to it, though," he said, his voice warming.

Electricity hummed between them as they stared at each ther. Jolie sucked in a wobbly breath. Then the hardness in organ's tone matched the accusation in his eyes.

"What are you doing here, Jolie? Why aren't you taming pids in some far-off place?"

"I…I'm—" She stumbled over her words. "I'm taking a ave from competition for a little while. I had a bad run in irginia." She couldn't bring herself to say that she'd almost ed. "Your dad offered me this teaching opportunity."

LIEXP0413RR

"I heard about the accident and I'm real sorry about that, Jolie," Morgan said. "But why come here after all this time?"

"This is my *home.*"

Jolie saw anger in Morgan's eyes. Well, he had a right to it, and more than a right to point it straight at her.

But she'd thought she'd prepared for it.

She was wrong.

"Morgan," Jolie said, almost as a whisper. "I'd hoped we could forget the past and move forward."

Heart pounding, she reached across the space between them and placed her hand on his arm. It was just a touch, but the feeling of connecting with Morgan McDermott again after so much time rocked her straight to her core, and suddenly she wasn't so sure coming home had been the right thing to do after all.

Will Morgan ever allow Jolie back into his life—and his heart?

Pick up HER UNFORGETTABLE COWBOY from Love Inspired Books.

LIEXP04